D.J. had automatically taken a deep breath when he sailed out of the raft and over the water. That lungful of air wouldn't last long. He had to breathe, but which way was up?

He tried to see light, indicating the sky, but he only saw millions of white bubbles, surging past his open eyes. His ears were filled with a continuous sucking sound.

The churning caused by the violent mixing of the two icy currents below the submerged rock kept D.J. suspended between the rocky bottom and the foaming surface. As he was whirled around and around, up, down, sideways, forward, and backward, D.J. could feel the cold seep through the insulation of his wet suit and into his body.

"I've got to get out of the water fast!"

LEE RODDY is a former staff writer and researcher for a movie production company. He lives in the Sierra Nevada Mountains of California and devotes his time to writing books and public speaking. He is a co-writer of the book which became the TV series, "The Life and Times of Grizzly Adams."

Born on an Illinois farm and reared on a California ranch, Lee Roddy grew up around hunters and trail hounds. As a boy, he began writing animal stories. He spent lots of time reading about dogs, horses, and other animals. These stories shaped his thinking and values before he went to Hollywood to write professionally. His Christian commitment later turned his writing talents to books like this one. This is the tenth book in the **D.J. Dillon Adventure Series.**

Escape Down the Raging Rapids

LEE RODDY

VICTOR BOOKS®

A DIVISION OF SCRIPTURE PRESS PUBLICATIONS INC.
USA CANADA ENGLAND

THE D.J. DILLON
ADVENTURE SERIES

3 4 5 6 7 8 9 10 Printing/Year 94 93 92

All Scripture quotations are from the *New American Standard Bible*, © the
Lockman Foundation 1960, 1962, 1963, 1968, 1971, 1972, 1973, 1975, 1977.

Library of Congress Catalog Card Number: 88-60207
ISBN: 0-89693-477-2

VICTOR BOOKS
A division of SP Publications, Inc.
        Wheaton, Illinois 60187

CONTENTS

To my first grandchild:
Patrick O'Shaughnessy Roddy,
born January 26, 1988,
to my son, Steve, and his wife, Katie.

ACKNOWLEDGMENT

I want to express my deep thanks to William McGinnis of Whitewater Voyages, P.O. Box 906, El Sobrante, California 94803, for his cooperation in providing resources for this book.

Bill, a veteran of nearly 30 years of whitewater rafting, not only granted me an extensive tape interview, but also supplied various written reference materials with permission to use them without cost. These included his 360-page book, *Whitewater Rafting,* and his other publications, "The Guide's Guide" and "Class V Briefing." Bill also supplied such helpful data as his full-color catalog-brochure and various newspaper clippings.

While the characters and events in this book are purely fictitious, the incidents are based on events that might happen. However, the author has taken literary license in depicting some situations to make the story more exciting. That includes having young boys ride rafts without proper supervision or signed release forms.

The author has tried hard to make the story about river rafting as authentic as possible; if there are any errors in fact, they are solely the author's responsibility.

LEE RODDY
Penn Valley, California

Chapter One

DANGER ON EVERY SIDE

D.J. Dillon was really running scared that Saturday morning in late June. He had seen a forest fire before, but never like this! He was also feeling guilty. It was his fault that he and his best friend were in such terrible danger.

The two boys ran single file in the dusty, three-feet wide forest service trail at the 7,000-foot level of California's Sierra Nevada Mountains. Finally, D.J.'s pounding heart and raspy breathing forced him to stop. He turned around as Alfred Milford slid to a halt behind him.

D.J. panted, "I can't figure out how the fires moved so fast!" He raised his eyes and squinted at the morning sun. It was a red ball through the smoke that was solid as rain clouds. The nearest flames were a couple of miles away, yet ash drifted like gray half-dollars through the air. The boy's eyes smarted so much that tears ran down his grimy cheeks. The sharp smell of smoke filled his nostrils and made him want to cough.

Behind his thick eyeglasses, Alfred blinked rapidly to ease the smarting sting in his eyes. "The wind came up suddenly and then shifted," he replied. "With hundreds of fires burning toward each other and then coming together, it looks as if the whole world's on fire." Both boys tugged on their green, long-billed "Sugarpine" caps, trying to screen their eyes from the smoke.

"It's real scary!" D.J. said softly. He pulled his handkerchief from the right hip pocket of his faded blue jeans. He poured some water from his army surplus canteen on the handkerchief. He tied it across his nose below the eyes. "I hope this keeps some of that smoke out of my lungs!"

"It's worth a try," Alfred said, doing the same thing.

In the darkness, two low-flying, twin-engine air tankers dropped their fire-retardant chemicals in pink cascades over a hot spot. White smoke boiled up where the blaze went out, but the remaining flames raced on. The yellow-winged tankers circled and headed back to the distant airport for more chemicals. They met a helicopter trailing a huge canvas bucket of water below on a long cable. The chopper headed for the drop zone ordered by the air commander.

"Looks as if the fires are between us and camp," Alfred said. He pushed his thick eyeglasses up higher on the bridge of his nose with his right thumb. "If they are, we'll be cut off!"

"We'll make it!" D.J. said with a conviction he didn't feel.

"We'd better!" his skinny friend replied. "Youth camp's over at noon. We don't want to miss our ride back to Stoney Ridge. No way can we walk sixty miles to get home."

D.J.'s blue eyes skimmed the horizon in every direction. There was a horseshoe-shaped ring of exploding, fiery evergreen trees on all sides except for one half-mile wide stretch straight ahead, and miles of open area behind them.

A dry-storm* two days before had caused hundreds of lightning strikes that set countless wildfires throughout the high country. The wind had come up with the dawn today, driving the flames at a racing speed up steep, remote canyons. As small, scattered fires met and merged, they grew bigger, devouring fir, cedar, and Jeffrey pine* like a red-and-yellow monster gone mad.

"It's my fault for getting us into this mess!" D.J. said with feeling. "I'm sure sorry I came back for this sweater I left behind on our hike yesterday!"

He flipped the sleeves of a dark green garment tied around his neck and hanging down his back. "But Two Mom wouldn't have liked it if I'd lost this! She bought it special for camp." D.J.'s mother was dead, and his father had remarried. Two Mom was the boy's stepmother.

"She'll like it even less if we don't get back safely!" Alfred replied. His hard breathing made his skinny ribs show through the green T-shirt with the white letters spelling out "Camp Sugarpine" on the front. D.J. had on a T-shirt exactly like it.

D.J.'s own breathing seemed easier now, but he wasn't any less scared. "It looks like we can't get back to camp the way we came. Let's see if we can find another way. Alfred, you climb up that hill over there to the right and take a look. I'll go up this hill on the left. Meet me

*You can find an explanation of the starred words under "Life in Stoney Ridge" on pages 126–129.

back here in a few minutes. OK?"

Alfred nodded and took off through the smelly mountain misery,* avoiding clumps of poison oak and sharp buck brush. He began to climb a mountain of broken granite boulders, careful that his tennis shoes didn't slip. He squinted to ease the glare off the glistening glacial polish.

Breathing through the wet handkerchief was hard. Alfred sucked the cloth into his mouth while gasping for breath. The hill was so steep that he had to crawl on his hands and knees. Perspiration formed on his forehead and slid down in streaks inside his glasses. The salty drops burned his eyes even more than the smoke.

He had a painful stitch in his side, and his lungs were aching as he collapsed at the summit of the bare granite boulders. Though his glasses were now heavily streaked with drying perspiration, he could see five ridges below him, one behind the other, extending into the distance.

Usually, tall conifers* stretched along those ridges and down canyons in peaceful beauty of pale blue-green. But not today. Every ridge was aflame. Every canyon was filled with smoke.

Hopefully, Alfred lowered his gaze to the nearest two canyons. Camp Sugarpine lay between them. He licked his lips which were dry with fear.

"We really *are* cut off!" he whispered. "Those two fires burned toward each other and joined up so we can't get back to camp!"

He thought of all the other young campers, the counselors, and the parents who had come to pick up their children, including his own parents and D.J.'s. They were probably all anxiously waiting in camp, looking in the direction D.J. and Alfred had gone at dawn. Those waiting must have known the two boys were trapped by the flames.

Another trickle of perspiration ran off Alfred's eyebrows and across his glasses. He pulled the wet handkerchief from his face, removed the glasses, and began cleaning them.

Alfred seemed to be looking around, but without his glasses, he couldn't see ten feet away. He did not notice a well-muscled man and a teenaged boy at the foot of the bare granite mountain 200 yards below. They cautiously stuck their heads out the door of an expensive summer home they had just burglarized.

The man was in his mid-twenties. He peered around with hard gray eyes. He was used to looking for the sheriff or his deputies because he grew marijuana at his home and was known to be a poacher* of bear and deer. But this week he was on a rare "vacation" from his secret hideout downriver near Summit City. He wore a sweat-stained, gray cowboy hat, blue denim jacket and pants, cowboy boots, and a huge belt buckle shaped like a skull.

"All clear, Tobin!" he announced. "You ready?"

"Yeah, let's go." Tobin, a stocky boy of about sixteen, was freckled on his face and bare forearms and had a gap between his two upper front teeth. He wore a faded red T-shirt, frayed cutoffs, tennis shoes without socks, and a brown leather hat. Tobin stopped in his tracks and said, "Before we go, let's burn this place."

"We haven't got time for that!" Odell growled, glancing around nervously. "We've got to get to the river or those rafters will leave without us."

"We got plenty of time!" Tobin lifted his homemade leather hat with a pheasant's long tail feather stuck in the band. He ran a freckled hand over his long, untidy reddish hair and resettled the hat on his head. "I want to see this place go up in smoke. The owner will think the forest fires did it."

"Forget it!"

"It'll only take me a minute to torch this place."

Tobin pulled a small box of matches from his cutoffs, removed one match, and struck it with his thumbnail. He bent and touched the flame to a dry Jeffrey pine branch on the ground. It flared into a crackling yellow blaze. The teenager picked up the other end of the branch and threw it onto the roof.

Odell swore mightily. He wouldn't admit it to anybody, but he had become afraid of his younger brother Tobin. Both were always in trouble with the law, but Tobin had a mean streak that tended to violence. He had gotten much worse since his last sentence in juvenile hall.

Odell muttered, "Why'd I have to have a crazy kid brother like you?"

Tobin grinned without humor. "You're just lucky, I guess. The guy who owned this place isn't. Maybe if he'd left something worth stealing, I wouldn't burn it— Oh! Look! There's a kid on top of that hill!"

The man swung around. Two hundred yards away sat Alfred in his *Camp Sugarpine* T-shirt and cap. He appeared to be watching Tobin and Odell. "He's looking in this direction too. He must've seen us come out of this place. Come on! Let's get out of here!" Odell turned toward the nearest stand of sheltering pines.

"But he can identify us!" Tobin yelled.

"No, he can't. He's too far away to get a good look at us. Besides, we'll never see him again!" the older brother called over his shoulder.

Reluctantly, Tobin trotted after Odell. "What if he reports us to a ranger or somebody?"

"There's no rangers around! Everybody's off fighting fires!"

"Well, if I ever meet up with that kid, he won't be able to identify *me* or anybody else ever again!"

"You're nuts, Tobin! You do him in, and you'll get more than 'juvie' hall* like before."

The brothers disappeared into the deep shadows of the towering conifers.

At the top of the hill, Alfred finished wiping his glasses. He blinked and rubbed his burning eyes. He couldn't see Tobin or Odell or anything that had happened at the bottom of the hill. He turned around, his back to the burning house. Sliding the glasses into place, Alfred pulled the wet handkerchief over his nose and mouth again, adjusted his cap, then scooted on the seat of his pants down the steep, slick granite mountainside.

Alfred rejoined D.J. at the bottom of the hill and the boys quickly compared their findings. The fires had cut them off from camp. A horseshoe-shaped line of fires burned on all sides except behind them.

D.J. swallowed hard, trying to ignore the familiar taste of fear. His mouth was dry and his tongue felt like a clapper in an old bell. "We've got no choice but to turn back and try to reach the river."

"But—everybody's waiting for us at camp! My folks, yours, Brother Paul—*everybody!*"

"I know that!" D.J. spoke more harshly than he wanted to. "But we can't get through that way, so we've got to go the only way we can!"

"Then what?" Alfred challenged.

"Remember those rafters we saw yesterday? They were getting ready for a run down Mad River. Maybe if they're still there, they'll give us a ride. And if they're not, at least there's a wide sandbar and lots of water. We'd be safe until the fire burns past us!"

"But if we don't get back to camp, everyone there will think we got burned to death!"

"We will be if we don't get to the river fast!" D.J. turned around and headed back the way they'd been.

Alfred moaned and started following. "If you hadn't left your sweater yesterday, we wouldn't be in this mess!"

D.J.'s guilt was so strong that he didn't reply right away. Quarreling wouldn't help them. D.J. tried to change the subject.

"I was in the camp lounge last night when I heard the Sacramento newscaster say that there are more than a thousand forest fires burning . . . *ouch!*"

D.J. reached down to slap hard at his blue jeans where they almost touched his dirty tennis shoes.

Alfred asked, "What's the matter?"

D.J. bent over and pulled up his pants leg. "Something bit me."

His blue eyes scanned the once-white crew sock now brown from the fine dust of the trail. His straight blond hair fell across his eyes as he examined the top of his sock and his bare leg. "I don't see anything, but—there!"

"What?"

D.J. raised his right foot to rest his tennis shoe on a small boulder surrounded by mountain misery. "A flea! Whoops! He got away."

"A *flea?*"

"You think a boy who's got a dog doesn't know a flea when he sees one? But where'd it come from?"

Alfred looked around and pointed to a small animal's burrow at the base of a large black oak just off the trail. "Probably from that dead ground squirrel there by its hole."

D.J. glanced down and nodded. "Yeah, probably so. Come on, let's get moving."

"Wait!" Alfred held up a restraining hand. "Look!" He pointed to a poster about six feet up the trunk of a nearby Jeffrey pine.

The bright yellow sign was about the size of a standard piece of paper the boys would use in school. At the top left, there was a black and white drawing of a chipmunk facing inch-tall red letters: **PLAGUE WARNING!**

D.J. wanted to be a writer when he grew up, so he was curious about almost everything. He stepped through the smelly mountain misery to better see the sign's smaller black letters. He read aloud:

"Chipmunks, ground squirrels, or other wild rodents in this area may be infected with plague. Plague may be transmitted to humans by the bite of an infected flea or by handling an infected animal."

D.J. suddenly stopped reading. "Oh, no!" he exclaimed softly, looking down where his pants leg now covered the fleabite. Then the boy raised his eyes and skimmed the rest of the poster.

"See a physician if you become ill. . . . " The rest of that line and the bottom of the sign had been torn off.

Alfred whispered, "Oh, boy!"

"*Plague?*" D.J. asked, jumping away from the tree and back onto the trail. "Isn't that like the Black Plague we read about in European history?"

At Stoney Ridge Elementary School, kids called Alfred "the Brain" because he read so much and remembered almost everything. He answered D.J.'s question. "Yes. Bubonic or Black Plague. During the middle 1300s, about 25 million people in Europe died from it."

"Wasn't it spread by rats?"

"Fleas, mostly from rats."

"That's a thing of the past, right? Whoever heard of anyone having the plague today?"

"That's because doctors know how to treat it. But that sign on the tree shows it's still around."

D.J. stood up and brushed off the back of his blue jeans. "How long does it take for the plague germs to—to—you know—"

"I was reading about it last week in a set of encyclopedias I got at a garage sale."

"How long?" D.J. asked anxiously.

Alfred hesitated, then answered quietly. "There are two kinds, as I remember. One takes about a week for a person to—die."

"And the other kind?" D.J. asked in a whisper.

"Three days."

D.J. stared in disbelief. "You mean—unless I get to a doctor fast, I may be dead in—three days?"

Alfred didn't answer.

"Alfred, I've *got* to find a doctor! Come on! Let's see if there's one in that group of rafters down at the river!"

Chapter Two

A HOWLING DOG

D.J. and Alfred hurried along the forest service trail toward Mad River. On the opposite side of the nearest mountain ridge, Odell and Tobin were jogging single file along a deer trail leading to the same destination.

Meanwhile, at Camp Sugarpine there was a rush to evacuate the camp before the fires reached it. Alfred's parents had not been able to come because their pickup truck broke down, so D.J.'s parents volunteered to bring Alfred back. Since neither boy had returned from their early morning hike, Dad Dillon was frantic.

He was a powerfully built logger with a huge chest that seemed out of proportion to his short legs. When he was riled, he scowled fearfully and looked very intimidating. He shouted at the young camp counselor, "How come you let those boys go out there?"

"Mr. Dillon, I've tried to tell you: your boy and his friend didn't ask permission. They just slipped out early. Besides, at the time, the wind hadn't come up and the fires weren't so big and close."

Hannah Dillon, whom D.J. called Two Mom, had blue eyes, short blonde hair, and a nervous way of letting her hands flutter. Now they were steady. She laid one gently on her husband's powerful arm. "Easy, Sam," she whispered. She raised her voice. "Don't mind my husband, young man. He doesn't mean anything personal. He's just upset because the boys are in such terrible danger."

Slowly, Dad Dillon nodded. It wasn't in his nature to apologize or say he was wrong. Instead, he nodded to the counselor and walked away with Two Mom. Their eyes sought vainly for a sign of D.J. and Alfred coming through the smoke and flames that were advancing over the hills.

Brother Paul Stagg hurried up, his saddle-colored cowboy boots raising a fine dust in the campground's pine needles. He had driven up from Stoney Ridge to bring back the kids he had brought up to camp a week ago. The lay pastor was trailed by D.J.'s nine-year-old stepsister, Priscilla.

Two Mom looked up hopefully at the lay preacher who served Stoney Ridge's community church. "What'd you find out?" she called.

Brother Paul's deep bass voice rumbled up from a giant chest like distant thunder. "They're trying to get the air commander on the radio to ask if he's seen the boys. But he's so busy directing all those planes and helicopters they can't get through to him."

Priscilla's face was tearstained. "They can't just leave D.J. out there to burn up!" she cried, clutching her mother's hand. "They just can't!"

Two Mom bent over and stroked the girl's unruly

hair. D.J. had often teased Pris about it, saying it looked like an eagle's nest that had fallen on a fence-post. "Pris, get hold of yourself! D.J. and Alfred are going to be all right!"

"But the fires—"

"Enough, Pris!" Dad Dillon's voice was firm. "Hannah, take her over to the office and see if they've learned anything on the Sacramento or Reno radio or television stations."

It wasn't his nature to say "please." He was a logger— plain, hardworking, and strong. Inside, he was feeling the terrible pain of knowing his only son was caught in the forest fires.

Brother Paul removed his dove-colored cowboy hat and ran a ham-sized hand over damp red-gold hair. He squinted at the smoky sky with concerned eyes. In embroidered cowboy shirt, jeans, boots, and hat, he stood nearly seven feet tall. "Sam, the good Lord's going to take care of those boys, you know."

D.J.'s father tried to nod, but he couldn't. "I shouldn't have let him come to camp," he said fiercely.

The lay pastor placed a hand firmly on the shorter man's powerfully muscled shoulders. "Don't you go blaming yourself, Sam! This here's a Christian camp, and your boy needed to be here, same as Alfred and all them other kids."

He jerked his chin toward a line of cars parked haphazardly on the narrow blacktop curved road that ran in front of the rustic camp headquarters. Parents were hurrying their children, hastily stuffing camp clothes, blankets, and toiletries into their vehicles. They had one goal: to get out of the fire area as fast as possible.

Dad Dillon felt a momentary anger. Fire officials had

ordered the camp evacuated. That wasn't too difficult since most parents had already driven in to pick up their children after the closing lunch. But to Sam Dillon, it seemed all those other parents were running away. They were rushing their children to safety, leaving him alone with the terrible fear that *his* boy might be dying in the approaching flames.

But I can't blame them, he thought. Aloud, he said to Brother Paul, "Did you get through to the Milfords awhile ago?"

"Since they don't have a phone, I left a message at the little store near where they live. By now, John and his wife should know about their son and yours."

Brother Paul turned and looked back into the stand of soaring conifers where green-painted cabins nestled unobtrusively in the forest. "I expect the Milfords are doing some mighty powerful praying about now."

Dad Dillon nodded. John Milford had worked in the lumber mill with him. Right now, praying was about all Alfred's parents could do.

Both Sam Dillon and Brother Paul fell silent, looking around at the smoke rising from the fast-approaching fires. The threatened camp rested in a small valley between two forest-covered mountain ridges.

The big lay preacher's voice rumbled again. "I wonder if Caleb's heard yet?" Caleb Dillon was Sam's father and D.J.'s grandfather.

Sam replied, "No, he probably doesn't know. He's got no neighbors nearby and no phone, you know. He won't listen to the radio because he hates the music played these days, and his TV's broken."

"It's just as well. He'd be frustrated if he knew and couldn't do anything to help D.J."

"He wanted to come pick up D.J., of course, but he had to stay with the dogs."

D.J. had a little hair-pulling bear dog* named Hero that he loved as only a boy can. Since Two Mom was allergic to dogs, Hero always slept outside the house when D.J. was home to care for him. When the boy was away, the dog had to be sent to Grandpa Dillon. He took care of Hero, along with his own dog, Stranger.

Sam took a slow breath, remembering the special bond that had developed between Grandpa Dillon and D.J. Though Dad Dillon would never admit it to anyone, he wished he and D.J. had the same closeness as the boy and grandfather had.

Brother Paul watched another car pull away from the curb, throwing up dry pine needles and fine dust in the hurry to get away. "I can just see Caleb now, sitting in his old rocking chair, holding his Irish shillelagh,* and talking to the dogs."

*   *   *   *   *

Two hours' drive down from Camp Sugarpine, Grandpa Dillon sat on the rickety front porch of his small frame house. He was thin as a piece of baling wire and slightly stoop-shouldered. He wore patched overalls with a blue shirt buttoned at the neck. The long sleeves were rolled up to his elbows.

He peered anxiously over the top of his wire-rimmed bifocals, past the surrounding ponderosas,* black oaks, and cedars toward the distant smoke. He had not heard the news, but he'd spent too many years in the mountains not to recognize signs of forest fires in the high country.

The old man lowered his watery blue eyes to the dogs at his feet. Stranger, a part pointer mixture, was asleep with his head on his forepaws. He was medium sized, mostly white with some splotches of black. He was not a good-looking dog, but Grandpa didn't care.

Hero, D.J.'s dog, was so ugly he was cute, as Pris had said. Hero was reddish brown, shaggy-haired, and stub-tailed. A long, funny black nose stuck out from his muzzle like a plum on a thumb. He had been restless all morning. He sat on his haunches, staring off toward the distant smoke.

The old man lightly touched his rubber-tipped cane to the splintery porch floor. "You know, dogs, I'm right glad D.J. and them other kids finished their week of camping. That smoke 'pears to me to be right about where they went. But if I cal'clate correct, they should have left for home right 'bout now."

He shifted uneasily in his old rocking chair, using the Irish shillelagh to ease his arthritic hip. Like many people who live alone, the old man talked aloud when no other human was around.

"Yessiree, you dogs are a'goin' to see D.J. purty soon! I recken ol' Hero here will jist about twist hisself in two from happiness. Stranger, you're more like me—we'll be mighty glad to see the boy, but we won't show it too much."

Suddenly, D.J.'s dog lifted his head and cocked it to one side. There was something spooky about the action that made the short hairs on Grandpa Dillon's bare forearms stand on end. It was especially scary because this was the second time it had happened this morning.

"What's the matter? What's wrong, Hero?"

The scruffy mutt was half hound, a quarter Airedale,

and a quarter Australian shepherd. But he was one hundred percent love when it came to D.J. Dillon.

Slowly, Hero stood and sniffed the wind, testing it, sensing something in it more than the smoke barely noticeable this far from the fires.

Grandpa shoved himself to his feet with the aid of his cane. "He's a'doin' it again!" He bent over the dog. "What is it, Hero?" Grandpa lightly touched the hairpuller's broad head.

The dog moved away, scarred ears perked, whining softly, staring into the distance.

Grandpa glanced at Stranger. His dog was still asleep, his head on his front paws.

Whatever it is, Grandpa mused thoughtfully, *it's not bothering Stranger none. But he's my dog, and that hair-pulling bear dog is all D.J.'s.*

Suddenly, Hero threw up his head and let out a mournful howl that spun Grandpa around. He felt the short hairs stand up on the back of his neck. Goosebumps crawled across his back, shoulders, and down his arms.

"Something's happened to D.J.!" Grandpa exclaimed. "Something terrible!"

Grandpa couldn't explain it, but he was absolutely sure he was right. From a lifetime of being around dogs, the old man had formed some strong opinions about mysterious bonds that sometimes exist between certain dogs and their masters, like Hero and D.J.

Hero finished a long, quavering howl, took a breath, and threw up his muzzle again. The dog's anguished cry carried across the hills and slowly died out in the distance.

Grandpa looked up at the sky, still blue but starting to

turn gray from the distant smoke. The goosebumps tingled on his arms as he began to pray.

"Lord, I don't know what it is, but something's happening to my grandson! I ain't one to ask You for a whole lot of things, You know, but take care of D.J.! Do it now, please! Amen."

* * * * *

In the high Sierras, over sixty miles away, D.J. suddenly stopped in the trail. Alfred nearly bumped into D.J. as he turned and looked behind them.

Alfred asked, "What's the matter?"

"I don't know." D.J. felt a little foolish saying it. He glanced all around. "Thought I heard something."

"Maybe a deer or bear running from the fires. Come on! Let's get to the river!"

D.J. nodded but stood still a few seconds, listening and looking. He saw nothing but the flames below.

On the top of a ridge to the right and a hundred yards or so away, Tobin stood shock still. He had climbed to the top of a ridge.

A few feet below him, Odell called softly. "What'd you see?"

"It's that kid again!" Tobin kept his voice down. "The one who saw us! But he's with another kid—wearing glasses."

"You sure?"

"Positive! They're both wearing the same kind of T-shirts, but the one who saw us didn't have glasses! They're heading for the river!"

It was a simple case of mistaken identity that would thrust D.J. into great danger, though neither he nor Alfred had seen Tobin or Odell.

Odell swore softly. "I told you not to burn that place! Now there's not only a witness, but he's probably told his friend! That means I'm in trouble too!"

"Aw, neither of them kids is going to give us any trouble! I guarantee that!"

"Let's hurry and beat them to the river! Maybe we can shove off with the rafters before those two get there!"

"For their sakes, I hope we do!" Tobin said grimly.

Chapter Three

A BOY'S TERRIBLE LONGING

D.J. was glad when he and Alfred started around the last curve in the forest trail leading down the canyon to Mad River. They'd been here before with their fellow campers, so the boys realized they were getting close. That made D.J.'s heart speed up in hope.

"We're almost there!" he called over his shoulder to Alfred, who was walking a few steps behind in the narrow forest service trail.

"Then we'd better take off these handkerchiefs. We don't want to come out of these woods looking like a couple of bandits."

"I just hope they're still there," D.J. replied, removing his handkerchief from his face. The cloth was dry now, but it wasn't needed as before. The smoke and fires were falling behind as the boys eased down the mountain into the river canyon.

D.J. was still fighting mixed emotions. The guilt seemed heavier now.

He thought, *If I hadn't been careless yesterday, I wouldn't have forgotten my sweater when we stopped for lunch. And this morning, I didn't follow the rules either. We shouldn't have left camp without getting permission from our counselor.*

Then he defended himself. *But how could we have known the wind was going to change and make the fires cut us off?*

Trying to ease his conscience didn't help much, especially now that he had made matters worse by getting the fleabite. D.J. wondered if the deadly black plague germs were starting to work inside his body. He wasn't quite so worried about the fires anymore because they were falling well behind, though still moving this way.

The boy's mind jumped to his parents. They'd probably be frantic with worry about now. *They must think I'm dead,* D.J. told himself. *And Alfred too.*

That thought made him feel even guiltier, so he tried to switch his thinking. *Hope Grandpa's OK. I miss him.* The boy thought a moment, then added, *Dad too.*

Something stiff and distant stood between him and his father. There never was the same warm, good feeling as existed between Grandpa and D.J.

D.J. had once asked Two Mom when she was patching his jeans, "Why doesn't Dad love me?"

"Why David Jonathan Dillon!" his stepmother had exclaimed. "Whatever gave you that silly idea?"

"He never says it—that's why."

"Your father's not the kind of man to show much emotion, D.J., but that doesn't mean he doesn't love you."

"Does he ever tell you he loves you?"

"Sometimes." Two Mom had sighed a little and gone

on with her sewing. D.J. had an idea Two Mom would have liked to hear the words more often from her husband.

The one thing in this world D.J. wanted was for his father to show he really loved him—to say it in plain English. It was a terrible longing that hurt deep down inside.

Alfred broke into his thoughts, "I hear the rapids! We're getting close now."

"I hear them too," D.J. replied. He was anxious to see if the rafters were still there. He'd learned yesterday that this was a staging area, or initial launch point for a trip, called a put-in. Everything was carried in on mules and horseback. The rafters had walked in. It would take them a full day to get the rafts inflated and all the gear stowed. There was a good chance the people wouldn't have shoved off yet. Maybe there'd be a doctor among them. Maybe.

Or maybe not. D.J. tried not to think of that, or the deadly plague germs possibly starting to build within his body. He forced his thoughts away from that terrible idea and back to how this whole adventure had started.

At church the last few weeks, Brother Paul had urged parents to send their kids to youth camp. Some families in the little logging community of Stoney Ridge didn't have cars or pickups that would climb the steep mountain roads. So Brother Paul had driven up with a carload of kids when camp opened. Kathy, his daughter, had wanted to attend, but she got a serious case of the flu the night before and had to stay home. Brother Paul had promised to return when camp ended and drive the same kids back to Stoney Ridge.

D.J. said to Alfred, "I'm sure Kathy's all right now,

and I imagine she and her father are at camp picking up kids. Brother Paul's probably talking to Dad about you and me too."

*   *   *   *   *

D.J. was partially right. Brother Paul, assisted by D.J.'s father, was loading the last of four kids and their camping gear into his car. Kathy had stayed home with her mother to leave more room in the car for kids returning from camp.

"Well, Sam," the lay preacher rumbled as he carefully closed the car door. The kids inside were strangely quiet. "Everybody's gone but you and me. I've got to get these young'uns home. You coming?"

"I'm going to send Hannah home with Pris, but I'll stay here as long as I can."

"Since they've ordered the camp evacuated, that probably won't be much longer."

"Maybe it'll be long enough. I keep hoping there'll be some news, or the boys will come walking out of those mountains."

"I'm right sorry to leave you like this, Sam, but these young people's folks'll be fretting about their safety. But before I go, I'd like to pray with you." Brother Paul reached out and laid a big hand on the other man's shoulder.

Dad Dillon bowed his head while the lay pastor prayed quietly but fervently.

When he had finished, Dad Dillon echoed the lay pastor's "Amen." They walked around the back of the car filled with young campers.

"Paul, something's been bothering me for a long time."

"What's that, Sam?"

Dad Dillon hesitated. It was obviously very hard for him to say what was on his mind. "Paul, do you ever tell your daughter that you love her?"

"Almost every day. It's important for Kathy to know how her mother and I feel about her."

"But doesn't she know by the way you act?"

The big man sensed something behind Sam Dillon's words. Brother Paul thought for a moment before answering. "No, she doesn't. Nobody does, really. Love is not only something you *do*—it's something you *say*."

Dad Dillon didn't answer. He looked toward the fires.

The big preacher's face changed slightly as he seemed to understand what was troubling the powerfully built logger. "You've never told D.J. you love him, have you?"

Dad Dillon lowered his eyes to stare unseeingly at the ground, but he did not speak.

Brother Paul's voice was barely a whisper, but it came out with a deep, bass sound that seemed to make the ground tremble a little. "Sam, did I ever tell you the story about my father's death?"

Dad Dillon looked up in surprise, wondering what that had to do with the present situation. "No, I don't think so."

"Remind me some time. It may help you. Well, I've got to get these kids out of here. Call me when you get home or if I can do anything. Tomorrow the whole church will pray for D.J. and Alfred and your families. Will you be there?"

"I don't rightly know yet, Paul. I'm going to make one last check of the office before having Hannah drive Pris home."

The two men shook hands. In a moment, Brother

Paul's sedan was moving out of the camp, leaving only the Dillon car and a few official vehicles. There was a terrible loneliness about the place. Only the wind moaned softly in the tall pines. Dad Dillon walked rapidly toward his wife and stepdaughter.

D.J.'s a smart boy, the father thought, trying to comfort himself. *So's Alfred. When they got cut off from camp, they must've headed for Mad River. They'll be safe there until the fires burn out.*

* * * * *

Miles away, D.J. and Alfred finished rounding the final curve in the forest. D.J.'s anxious blue eyes probed ahead, straining to see through the last of the trees to the river where the rafters would be.

Alfred moved up to walk beside D.J. as the trail widened, and they came even with the last stands of trees.

Both boys were breathing hard, partly from running and partly from excitement and hope. They stepped out of the sheltering woods and gazed upon an acre or so of gravel with the river beyond. Steep granite cliffs rose sharply on the far side of the river.

D.J. let out a happy yelp. "Look! They're still here!"

Alfred grinned broadly. "Sure are! We made it! Let's hope there's a doctor among them!"

The boys ran across the open gravel bar, squinting against the sun's glare off the white rocks. The river in front of them was wide, quiet, and deep though the rapids could be heard upstream. Great boulders the size of two-car garages stuck up out of the river. They looked like giant prehistoric dinosaur bones whitened by the sun. The water was so clear the rocky bottom was visible.

Alfred puffed above the sound of the stones under their feet, "Are you going to tell them about the flea-bite?"

"Not unless I have to. First, I'm going to see if one of them is a doctor or a nurse. If not, I'll ask if anyone's got a CB radio,* a walkie-talkie* or some way of signaling an air tanker or helicopter if one flies over."

"If they can contact a helicopter by radio, maybe it can land and pick you up," Alfred said hopefully. "It'd take you right to the doctor. And maybe it could even get a message to our parents."

"I haven't seen any choppers or planes in the last half-hour or so. Maybe they had to land because it was too dangerous to fly anymore today."

"If none of those plans work, then what?"

"Maybe we'll get a ride down the river with the rafters. They could let me off at the first town. Hey—they've seen us! Everybody's looking over here!"

"I count eight people, including two women and a girl about our age. Look—they're waving!"

All but two of the people near the two beached rafts waved to the approaching boys. But not Tobin and Odell. They stood a few feet beyond the second raft, watching uneasily.

Tobin muttered, "It's those same two kids. The one without the glasses saw us burn that house!"

Tobin had no idea that he had the boys mixed up be-cause Alfred had removed his glasses to clean them when Tobin saw him.

Odell protested, "Hey, *I* didn't burn it!"

"You're just as guilty as I am! We both broke into that place. Anyway, I'm not going to let them send me back to that kids' jail!"

"Now how're you going to avoid it, Mr. Smarty?"

"I don't know yet. But I'll figure it out. Then those kids will wish they'd never come here!"

Chapter Four

AN UNSPOKEN THREAT

D.J. and Alfred had run about halfway across the acre of gravel when D.J. panted, "See that man with the beard? I'll bet he's a doctor."

"I sure hope so."

"And even if he isn't, we'll at least be safe from the fires because there's nothing to burn here. We can stay in the water until the danger passes if we have to."

A tall, good-looking man wearing blue jeans and a white T-shirt left the others, accompanied by a woman. He appeared to be in his late thirties. She looked to be in her late twenties, and was deeply tanned. She wore a red bandana tied over her short blonde hair. The couple hurried to meet D.J. and Alfred.

"Hi!" D.J. called, waving again. His hopes soared as the couple approached. D.J. called, "Boy, are we glad to see you! We saw you yesterday when we were hiking with Camp Sugarpine kids. I forgot my sweater when we stopped for lunch, so Alfred and I went back for it this morning, but the fires cut us off from camp."

The slender man returned D.J.'s smile. "I'm sorry about your problems, but welcome to our camp. I'm Brad Thurston, owner of the rafting company and chief guide for the trip. This is Connie Gainer—she's the guide and captain of the other boat."

"I'm D.J. Dillon and this is my friend, Alfred Milford."

They shook hands all around as Alfred explained, "When the wind changed and the fires cut us off from Camp Sugarpine, we figured the river would be the safest place until the fires burn themselves out."

"Safest place is to go downriver with us," Brad replied with a warm smile. "You qualified on Class Five rivers?"

"What's Class Five?" D.J. asked.

Brad's smile widened. "You just answered my question: you're not experienced on the most difficult rivers for rafting."

"Too bad!" Connie said. "We're shorthanded for paddlers."

Brad explained, "If you were qualified on this class river, you'd be welcome. Apparently, some of our party got cut off by the fires. They signed up for this trip but haven't shown up. We're already late and we've waited about as long as we can."

Connie nodded. "We're about to shove off. That man and the teenager with him just barely made it." She turned and pointed. "Odell and Tobin Swazey. They're brothers—Odell's the older. They said they were delayed by the fires too. Haven't been here more'n ten minutes or so."

D.J. asked, "How can you go down the river when there are so many wildfires burning out of control?"

"Easy!" Brad replied, pointing to the far bank. "See those cliffs? Solid granite! It's pretty much like that for a hundred miles. Oh, there are places where some trees and brush grow, but mostly the walls on both sides of the river are bare rock. They can't burn!"

"A hundred miles?" Alfred asked in surprise.

"This is a strange river, boys. It's entirely in a primitive wilderness area. Once you start downriver, you can't stop and you certainly can't turn back. It's sort of like a roller coaster, except much, much longer and scarier—but fun!"

Brad continued, "There's no way out except maybe by helicopter at certain camps—that's what we call the places where we stop for the night—and there are no roads or anything else in or out of the river. It's a rafting voyage nobody ever forgets!"

At the river, the Swazey brothers pretended to be busy with one of the rafts, but their suspicious eyes were on D.J., Alfred, and the two rafting guides.

"Did you see her point at us?" Odell hissed. "You dumb kid! Now look what you've done!"

"The kid's not pointing us out—*she* is! So maybe she's telling them we just got here!"

"Yeah, and maybe the boys are telling her about you burning down that house!"

"So what if they are—it don't make no difference. We could jump in this raft and shove off right now. There's plenty of grub. They'd be too surprised to stop us. We'd get away clean!"

"You're talking stupid! This is a Class Five river; the meanest, roughest, wildest kind there is anywhere! Even with our years of rafting experience, the two of us couldn't handle this raft alone!"

Tobin considered that reality, then smiled crookedly. "First chance I get, I'm gonna warn them kids to keep quiet. But even if they did tell on us, nobody can do anything until we get to a town where there's some law. So if those two kids go with us, maybe they can have an 'accident.' "

"An accident?"

"Sure—a bad one! Without witnesses, nobody can prove we burned down that place. No witnesses, nobody to testify against us."

"Stop saying *we* burned that place!"

"Well, you were there—that makes you just as guilty as me."

"No, it doesn't!"

"Oh, yes it does. And I intend to do something about the witnesses."

"I can't believe you'd be dumb enough to hurt those kids."

"I told you, it'd be an *accident!* We'll be in the clear—and we won't have to worry about those two kids ever again."

Odell didn't say anything more. He stared suspiciously at his younger brother and was afraid. Something really strange had happened to Tobin in the last year or so. Odell didn't like it. He feared that Tobin's anger and hatred now directed against the two boys could be used against an older brother. Odell feared that he could be in just as great a danger as the boys.

In the middle of the gravel bar, D.J. and Alfred were getting acquainted with Brad and Connie.

Connie said, "Well, you boys are probably ready for a cool drink and something to eat. Come on down to the rafts and I'll get you both something."

D.J. smiled his thanks. "Alfred, you go ahead. I want to talk with Mr. Thurston a moment."

Alfred walked off with the girl guide, leaving D.J. alone with Brad.

"Mr. Thurston, I need to ask you something."

"Call me Brad."

"OK—Brad. Is there a doctor or nurse in your group?"

"That one with the beard's called 'doctor,' but he's with a college or something. A Ph.D.—Doctor of Philosophy. He's not a medical doctor. Why? Got a problem?"

"Something bit me a few hours ago. An insect. It doesn't hurt, but I'd kind of like to have it looked at."

Brad turned, cupped his hands over his mouth, and called, "Connie, bring the first aid kit, please!"

D.J. said, "Thanks. Anybody got a walkie-talkie, CB radio, or something like that?"

"I'm sorry; no. I can understand how worried you boys would be about calling your parents, but there's no way to do that from here. Nobody's going in or out of this place until those fires burn past, and that may take days."

D.J. kicked a small pebble with his tennis shoe. "I see."

"D.J., is there any chance that someone from your camp would come looking for you?"

"Nobody could get through the fires. The only search would have to be from the air, but we've noticed that all the planes and helicopters have stopped flying over. Nobody's going to spot us today, I guess."

Connie approached with the first aid kit, a sandwich, and a can of cold soda. Alfred followed her, munching on a sandwich and sipping from his soft drink can.

Connie handed the food and drink to D.J. and asked, "You got a scratch or something?"

D.J. sat down on an old log near the riverbank. "Insect bite," he said, pulling up his pants leg.

"I'll put some antiseptic and a bandage on it," Connie said. "You enjoy this sandwich and soda."

D.J. was surprised how hungry he was. He'd long ago finished the water in his canteen, so he ate and drank in silence while Connie worked. It only took her a moment. D.J. thanked her. She smiled and headed back to the rafts alone. Alfred stayed with D.J. and Brad.

The chief guide had also been silent. Now he asked quietly, "What bit you?"

D.J. hesitated, looking at Alfred, who nodded. D.J. explained. "A flea. Probably came off a dead ground squirrel."

Brad leaned down to look the boy squarely in the eyes. "You've seen the plague signs, haven't you, and you're scared?"

"We saw part of a sign. The rest had been torn off."

Brad nodded. "It just so happens we had the same problem some years back. There were lots of signs posted, and they scared my passengers. So I studied up on the subject.

"There are two kinds of plague: one's called pneumonic, and the other is black plague. The first kind is highly communicable. That means it can be transmitted from person to person, and it kills fast—in less than three days."

Alfred gasped. "Contagious—of course! I should have known!"

D.J. was so surprised he could barely speak. "You mean—I could spread it to Alfred and you and all these other people? We could all die within a few days?"

"You didn't let me finish," Brad protested. "That's the pneumonic kind. But the other is only transmitted by a fleabite."

D.J. frowned, not sure he understood.

Brad explained, "Even if the flea that bit you was carrying the plague germs, you can't pass the disease to Alfred or me or anyone.

"In fact, D.J., you're the only one who's in danger. You can't infect anyone, but you can die if you don't get medical treatment. The plague incubation period* from a fleabite is about a week.

"If I remember those signs correctly, they say something like, 'See a physician if you become ill within a week. The disease is curable when diagnosed early.' "

Alfred exclaimed, "That part was missing on the sign we saw."

"D.J.," Brad continued, "you said you were bitten this morning. So if you *are* infected, you've got a week to see a doctor."

"But the only way I can get to a doctor is by going downriver with you to the nearest town, and you won't take me!"

"Try to see it from my side, D.J. I'd face a double risk. You're not experienced in rafts, and suppose you get too sick to paddle or even to sit up in the boat?"

Alfred said quickly, "I'll take care of him."

"That's noble of you, Alfred," the guide replied, "but you're inexperienced in rafts too. I could have a real tough situation on my hands."

D.J. grabbed at a thought. "How long's your trip going to take?"

"Three days."

"How far are we from the first town?"

"We go right near Summit City in two days."

"Do they have a doctor there?"

"Yes, of course. Oh, I see what you mean. This is Saturday. So we should be at Summit City about Monday afternoon. We should be able to get you there well before the incubation period is over."

D.J. asked hopefully, "Then you'll take us? Our fathers will pay you when they come to pick us up!"

The guide hesitated a moment, studying the boys' anxious faces. "OK, on two conditions. First, not a word of this to anybody else, not even Connie. She works for me, so she'll do anything I say, but I don't want to scare people even though they're perfectly safe from the disease."

"Fine!" D.J. cried.

"I also want you both to get some quick lessons in rafting before we shove off. Agreed?"

"Sure!" Both boys said it together.

"Then let's meet the others so we can get started."

Brad led D.J. and Alfred toward the first raft and introduced them to the rafters. D.J. tried to remember their names.

The bearded man was Dr. George Trotman, an associate professor at the state university in Sacramento. The girl was his daughter, Renee.

"Hi," she said, smiling at both boys. She wore a blue tank top blouse, cut-off blue jeans, and gray tennis shoes. She was not very tall, with short dark hair and brown eyes. Her tanned bare arms showed she was an outdoor girl. "Glad to have some boys along who are my age."

Her father nodded. "Boys, glad you could join us."

As Brad led the boys to the next rafters, D.J. was surprised to feel Alfred nudge him and whisper, "She's going to be fun!" D.J. blinked. He'd never heard his best friend say anything before about any girl.

One man stood by himself, staring into the river. He turned slowly when Brad called, "Ray, meet another couple of our late crew members. Ray Hazelbury, this is D.J. Dillon and Alfred Milford."

Ray did not smile. He looked like a piece of well-used rawhide, thin but strong. He had an old scar above his right eye and a sour look on his long, thin face. "Hello," he said. He did not offer to shake hands. He turned to stare at the river.

"Don't mind him," Brad whispered to the boys as they moved on. "Some people just aren't as friendly as others."

Toni Horner was next. She was in her late twenties, D.J. guessed. She wore her short ash blonde hair in a pixie haircut. She was a big woman, close to six feet, and an obvious outdoor type. Her handshake was firm, almost hard. "Welcome to the adventure of your lives, boys!"

Brad led the boys toward the last two members of the rafting party. "Tobin and Odell Swazey, here are another couple of latecomers who had a close call with the fires."

The older brother straighened up, brushed his hands against his pants, then reached out to shake hands with D.J. and Alfred. "Glad to know you boys. I'm Odell. He's my kid brother, Tobin."

The sixteen-year-old Tobin held a six-foot hardwood maple paddle. He did not offer to shake hands. Instead, he shoved the blade of the paddle toward the boys, touching their hands rapidly in turn with the tip. Then, without a word or even a nod, he turned and started working on the raft again.

As Brad, D.J., and Alfred moved away, Alfred said softly, "That's the first time I ever shook hands with an oar!"

"Paddle," Brad corrected. "We don't have any oars on these rafts. You'll learn all the terms pretty soon, just as all the people will learn to know and like each other. Rafting has a way of bringing people together.

"Except for the Trotman and Swazey family members, everyone else is a stranger. But soon they'll all be like one big happy family. You'll see. Now let's go outfit you boys with wet suits, life jackets, and crash helmets. I'll have to stow your hats and that sweater."

D.J. glanced at the Swazey brothers. The older one was bent over the raft, but Tobin stared at D.J. with cold eyes. Tobin's lips moved, forming soundless words. D.J. couldn't read them, yet he had the strangest feeling Tobin was threatening him. But why?

Chapter Five

A WARNING ON THE RIVER

In a few minutes, D.J. learned more about the wordless
threat he'd seen Tobin mouth.

With Alfred's glasses securely tied on, both boys carried black wet suits, orange life jackets, and yellow helmets upstream to where Connie was giving the basic
rafting instructions.

The wet suits were tight-fitting, insulated, and rubberized garments that covered the body from wrist to
neck to ankles against the numbing water temperature
of 50 to 55 degrees. Some rafters also had insulated boo-
ties, but D.J. and Alfred wore their tennis shoes.

The brightly colored life preservers were like sleeve-
less jackets with clasps in front for putting on or removing. The buoyant vest-like items were to keep a person
afloat if swept overboard. Brad and Connie each had
two special knives in sheaths on the shoulders of their
life jackets.

All the rafters wore helmets fitted close to the head to

protect against accidental blows from another rafter's paddle, or injury to heads banged against rocks if a rafter was swept overboard.

D.J. and Alfred came to where Connie was working in the water with some of the other rafters in a section of quiet water below the rapids. D.J. and Alfred sat on the riverbank and got into their outfits while watching Connie review with four crew members the way to right a raft which had been deliberately overturned in the river.

The Swazey brothers walked up, carrying their rafting outfits. Brad had apparently sent them to Connie for a quick review of the basics though they claimed to be expert rafters.

D.J. looked up from where he was sitting on the riverbank, struggling into the wet suit. Tobin bent down while his brother kept walking upstream.

"Hey, you!" Tobin's voice was sharp but low.

D.J. glanced up. "You talking to me?"

"Well, I'm not talking to your four-eyed friend! He looks like an owl trying to see through the bottom of a soda pop bottle."

D.J. and Alfred exchanged concerned glances. D.J. looked up at Tobin. "I'm D.J. and he's Alfred."

"Who cares?" Tobin snapped. "I saw you talking to Brad alone! Did you tell him?"

D.J. was totally confused. The only thing Tobin might be talking about was the fleabite, but Tobin couldn't know about that. D.J. said, "I don't know what you're talking about."

"Don't play games with me!" Tobin leaned down so his face was within a foot of D.J.'s. "Did you tell or not?"

Again, D.J. and Alfred exchanged glances. Both were

totally puzzled by Tobin's questions.

D.J. said to Tobin, "Neither of us has told anybody about anything because—"

"Keep it that way!" Tobin interrupted. "If either of you opens your mouth, you'll be sorry! Remember that!" He straightened up and ran after his older brother.

The friends stared after the sixteen-year-old boy. Alfred asked softly, "What was that all about?"

"Beats me. A little while ago, I thought he mouthed some threatening words at me. But I've never seen him or his brother before."

"Guess he's got you mixed up with somebody else. Boy! I hope we aren't going to have trouble with him."

"We'll straighten that out later. Come on—Connie's motioning for us. Let's go get some instructions about rafting."

Feeling strange in their wet suits and tennis shoes, the boys carried their helmets and life preservers upstream. They had expected to see the rapids which they could hear, but Connie was below the rapids in a wide, quiet section of the river with one raft and some of the crew. D.J. recognized the bearded Dr. Trotman, Odell Swazey, the sour-faced Ray Hazelbury, and the other woman, Toni.

Renee Trotman sat on the bank with Tobin. She waved D.J. and Alfred over. "Come sit down! Connie's giving practice in righting a flipped raft."

Tobin scowled up at the two boys. D.J. wished that he didn't have to go downriver with somebody who seemed mad at him for some unknown reason. D.J. squatted down, hoping to be able to show Tobin he and Alfred were friendly.

D.J.'s emotions were all mixed up. He didn't like having Tobin upset with him, but mostly he was wishing they were on their way downriver toward a doctor. And D.J. was concerned about how his family was doing.

D.J. looked at the people in the water, but he wasn't really seeing them. Instead, in his mind, he was seeing Stoney Ridge, Grandpa, and Hero. By now, word would have come about what had happened to D.J. and Alfred in the forest fires.

*   *   *   *   *

Standing on the front porch of his small frame house, resting on his Irish shillelagh, Grandpa Dillon looked in disbelief at Brother Paul and his daughter. They'd driven out to bring the old man the news.

Grandpa asked softly, "You mean to stand there and tell me D.J.'s dead in that there forest fire?"

"No, Caleb, I didn't *say* that!" the lay pastor protested in his deep, booming voice. "I just said that the boys got caught in the fire when the wind sprang up suddenly and shifted direction!"

Kathy added quickly, "We're sure D.J. and Alfred'll be all right, Brother Dillon." Kathy was very slender and tall for her age. She had her father's blue eyes, reddish-gold hair, and lots of freckles.

Grandpa stared silently at his visitors, the fear and pain starting to show in his watery blue eyes. He turned and looked down at Hero. After greeting the Staggs, the dog had returned to his vigil at the edge of the porch. He sat on his haunches, his eyes fixed on the distant, smoky sky.

Grandpa mused, "So that's what got into D.J.'s dog!" He briefly told the father and daughter about Hero's howling and strange behavior that morning. Grandpa added, "But he's still a'watchin', and he ain't howled none since, so I recken D.J.'s still all right, somewhar."

Brother Paul saw an opportunity to give the old man hope. "Of course he is! Look at that dog—Hero looks like he expects to see D.J. coming up the hill from the crick* any second!"

"He sure does," Kathy agreed. She echoed something she had often heard adults say at church. "You just got to have faith, Brother Dillon."

Slowly, the old man nodded. He shifted his grip on his cane and limped over to stand beside the ugly little mutt that loved his grandson as much as he did. "Hero, I betcha D.J.'s done found a way to get out of that there forest fire! I don't know how, but I recken he's a'gettin' ready to come out right now!"

*   *   *   *   *

Back at the river, D.J. was vaguely aware that Alfred and Renee were talking, but D.J. wasn't really listening.

"Oh! Watch!" Renee grabbed D.J.'s arm so his attention shifted from thinking about Grandpa and Hero to the river in front of them.

The four passengers under Connie's instructions had deliberately flipped the raft over. In helmets, life jackets, and wet suits, they scrambled out of the icy water and onto the upside-down raft. They quickly righted it and crawled in, yelling happily with the accomplishment.

"Yea!" Renee cried, applauding happily. "Great work, Dad! Our turn next," Renee said as Connie instructed the rafters to paddle toward the shore.

Renee turned to D.J. and Alfred. "How many years

have you two been rafting?"

"Uh—this is our first time," D.J. answered.

Tobin sputtered, "Your first—? How come they let you do that? This is my *sixth* year. Why, you dumb clucks could get us all drowned!"

Renee protested, "Oh, Tobin, don't be such an old grouch. It's obvious that Brad can't leave D.J. and Alfred here. The fire would get them!"

D.J. looked at the girl and smiled. "Thanks."

"This is my fifth year," Renee said. "I'll help give you boys some pointers if you want."

"We want!" Alfred cried. "Thanks!"

D.J. nodded in agreement, but his eyes went to Tobin. His face was dark with anger and resentment. D.J. felt very uneasy and hoped he wouldn't be in the same raft with Tobin.

Alfred said, "D.J.'s going to be an author someday, so he likes to know all kinds of things."

"An author?" Renee asked, smiling broadly at D.J. "Have you written anything yet?"

"Just some stories for the local newspaper plus an article for a national magazine."

Renee stood up as the raft touched shore. "Then I'll help teach you about rafting and maybe someday you'll dedicate a book to me."

Tobin, D.J., and Alfred stood and headed for the raft. Renee explained, "The raft is sixteen feet long and eight feet wide. Notice that it has a slightly upturned bow— that's the front end. The back is called the stern."

D.J. studied the raft more closely as Renee's explanation continued. The raft was a soft blue color with a black strip at the waterline. A yellow rope, called a line, ran along the entire outside of the twenty-inch buoyancy tubes that circled the raft. Though the rafts were called "ten man" boats, a load of four to six people per craft was considered plenty for rafting. Since some scheduled passengers hadn't shown up, there would be only four crew members per boat with Brad in charge of the lead boat and Connie in the second, called the sweep.

Renee continued, "See the paddles they're using? They're not oars, but paddles. You never let go of your paddle! That's a rule! Even when you're washed overboard or the raft flips, try to hang on to your paddle!"

Tobin growled, "Aw, Renee! Don't tell them all that stuff!"

"It's fun!" Renee replied cheerfully.

D.J. was impatient to be on his way downstream, away from the fires and toward a doctor. Still, he recognized the need to learn as much about rafting as possible. When his turn came to be instructed by Connie, he tried hard to keep his mind on what she said.

The blood-red sun, riding above the smoky skies, was nearly overhead when Connie waved D.J. ashore and praised him.

"D.J., you did a good job of using your feet to push off from that boulder just now! The rest of you remember to do what he did. If you're washed overboard, always point your feet downstream. Keep the toes just barely breaking the surface. Use your feet to keep from getting smashed against the rocks! If you drag your feet, especially in shallow water, you can get what's called 'foot entrapment.' People have drowned from that. All right, everyone! Let's go tell Brad we're ready to start our run down the raging rapids!"

D.J. was really happy to be on the way. He grinned at Alfred and Renee as they hurried along the bank, carrying their four-and-a-half-foot softwood spruce paddles.

Renee explained, "Usually, the most experienced crew is in the first boat. But because D.J. and Alfred are short on practice, they'll probably divide us up a little differently. I sure hope to be in the same raft with you two."

"Thanks!" Alfred replied with a big grin.

D.J. started to agree, then glanced at Tobin. His eyes were narrowed, and a hard look had settled over his face. D.J. hoped they wouldn't be assigned to the same craft.

His thoughts were interrupted by Brad's instructions. "Listen carefully," he began. "I've got to give you my world-famous talk on rafting safety." He said this with a smile which was returned by the rafters. Then he talked about various situations that could develop.

D.J. paid careful attention to the "man overboard" instructions. The guide said it wasn't uncommon for a person to be swept overboard in rough water, but danger was minimized by remembering how to act if that happened.

Finally, Brad gave instructions on where each rafter was to ride down the river. "I'll be the captain and take the stern of the first boat. Dr. Trotman—I mean, George—you take the right bow position. Ray, you've got the left. Toni, you're behind Ray. Alfred, let's put you behind George. That's five in our lead boat. The rest of you take the positions Connie assigns you in the sweep, or second boat."

D.J.'s heart took a jump. That meant Tobin and Odell would be in the boat with him, and he'd be separated from his best friend.

Connie took the stern position with the gear carefully

stowed at her feet.

All equipment needed on the trip was divided between the two rafts. In each raft the gear was behind the paddlers and right in front of the boat captain. Items included cooking utensils, food, bedding, and tents. Everything was protected with waterproof coverings and securely lashed down with ropes at the captain's feet.

Connie gave D.J. the right bow position with Odell opposite him. That put Renee behind Odell and Tobin behind D.J. This made him very uneasy. Still, there was no way he could logically ask Connie to change their positions.

D.J. settled into the raft, carefully wedging his knees under the rope thwarts* as he had been taught. He held onto his blue-handled oar with the yellow blade and waited anxiously to start.

The lead boat with Brad, Ray, Toni, Alfred, and Renee's father shoved off downstream.

Connie seemed to sense D.J.'s uneasiness. She said, "It'll take you a while to get used to the commands, but they'll soon be second nature." She raised her voice slightly and gave the first command. "Forward!"

He remembered to keep his inboard hand on top of the paddle grip and the outboard hand away down on the shaft, just above the blade.

D.J. dug his paddle into the water. It came up fast, splashing water everywhere. Tobin yelled in protest. "You're drowning me!"

D.J. apologized, but Connie said with a chuckle, "Boys, you can't ride a raft without getting a little wet! OK, we're on our way!"

D.J. was glad about that. He brought the paddle down wrong again. It hit almost flat instead of digging into the water. This time the resulting splash sailed across the bow and splattered Odell.

"Hey!" he yelled. "Watch it, kid!"

"Sorry!" D.J. muttered, trying to control the paddle.

Suddenly, D.J. did it again. His paddle hit wrong, sending icy water into the raft behind him.

Tobin leaned forward and whispered, "You're in *big* trouble!"

D.J. apologized, but he knew that wasn't going to do any good. He already had enough troubles, but he was heading for still more.

They came sooner than he expected.

Chapter Six

MAN OVERBOARD!

Before shoving off, Brad had said the two rafts would run down the river about an hour and stop for a late lunch. The river was fairly smooth, so D.J. had time to adjust gradually to rafting. At first, he was uncomfortable in his yellow helmet, orange life vest, and black wet suit, but he knew they were necessary and began to get used to them.

As he learned to control his paddle better, he also relaxed and enjoyed the experience somewhat.

It was pretty in the canyon. He saw a doe with her speckled fawn bounding away from where they'd been drinking from the river. Once D.J. glimpsed a sow bear with her cub back up in the brush. He remembered the bear cub he had owned for a while and wondered how Koko* was doing now.

Everything was peaceful in the river.

The forest fires slowly disappeared from view. The wind blew the smoke the other direction, so D.J. saw nearly clear skies again.

Yet, in spite of the tranquillity, D.J. had a gnawing sense of danger. It wasn't just from the fleabite and the possibility that deadly black plague germs were multiplying inside his body. The feeling of being in jeopardy was more immediate.

D.J. thought, *I wonder why Tobin's got it in for me? Maybe he's got me mixed up with somebody else. But who?*

D.J. thought again of the mess he'd gotten himself and his best friend into. He had apologized to Alfred, but he still felt guilty about slipping off to get his sweater without asking permission. D.J. raised his eyes and said a silent prayer.

Lord, I'm sorry about doing a wrong thing in leaving camp without permission. I'm sorry! I won't do it again. Please take away my guilt so I can think about what to do now.

The boy sighed, feeling better. The fires were no danger to the boys now. The fleabite still posed a health threat, but D.J. figured he'd reach a doctor in plenty of time for antiplague treatment. That left the river and Tobin's strange behavior for D.J. to be concerned about. And his family! They were probably suffering terribly right now, thinking D.J. and Alfred were trapped in the fires.

I wonder what Dad's doing, the boy mused, arms stroking automatically with the paddle. *I wonder what he's thinking.*

*   *   *   *   *

Dad Dillon had been forced to leave the evacuated

Camp Sugarpine as the forest fires burned closer. He got a ride with a ranger in his pickup to the main highway that led back down to Stoney Ridge.

"Look," Dad Dillon said as the ranger's pickup slowed on a graveled shoulder, "I can't go back home when my boy's out there somewhere." He waved a work-hardened hand toward the surrounding fires. "Give me a hard hat and a shovel or something and let me go in with the hand crews to fight this thing!"

The ranger's long, thin face was already showing signs of having been on the fire line for days. He shook his head. "Sorry, Mister, we're not calling for local volunteers."

"But I'm a lumberman! I've fought forest fires before!"

"And you may be called on to do it again, but not now. A few minutes ago on my radio I heard that two people died this morning fighting these fires—two experienced fire fighters! There'll probably be more before this thing is over! Please—go home for now."

Dad Dillon fell silent as the pickup's tires crunched along the shoulder gravel and stopped. "But I can't just do nothing!" he cried, turning imploring blue eyes upon the ranger. "I've *got* to help!"

"You'll help everybody the most by going home to the rest of your family!" He softened his tone to add, "You can't help your boy, but you can help your wife and daughter. Sorry I can't help you otherwise, Mister."

Dad Dillon reluctantly opened the passenger-side door and stepped out. "Much obliged," he said.

The ranger's pickup pulled away, its long radio antenna whipping in the air. Dad Dillon stood beside the highway that stretched like a string through the tall timber. The road was strangely silent since most traffic had been diverted around the fire danger zone.

Dad looked up at the magnificent pines that rose eighty to a hundred feet into the smoky sky. He looked beyond their graceful tips. Dad's lips moved, but he spoke only in his heart.

Lord, I'm just a logger, and I don't have the words. All I got's a terrible pain inside because my boy's out there, somewhere, and I can't help him. Show me what to do, please!

His eyes were suspiciously bright after his short prayer. He was only vaguely conscious of a four-wheel drive vehicle passing, then braking suddenly. Dad looked up as the four-wheeler backed up even with him.

The small, wiry driver leaned across the front seat and called through the open passenger-side window. "Sam? Is that you?"

"Hello, Red. Yeah, it's me." Red Garn was a member of Stoney Ridge's only church. He had been fishing at one of the remote lakes, so was late in escaping the fires.

"What're you doing out here in the middle of no-where? Your car break down?"

Dad shook his head. "I sent my wife home with the car after my boy wandered away from camp with his friend, Alfred Milford. The fires must have cut them off. They—haven't come back."

"Oh, Sam! I'm mighty sorry! Can I help?"

The logger shook his head. "No, thanks. They won't even let *me* help. Told me to go home."

"Get in and I'll give you a ride."

Dad stood a moment in silence, listening to the wind sigh in the treetops and watching the smoke curl up from the surrounding fires. "Much obliged," he said, and climbed into the four-wheeler. "I recken it is a bad time for Hannah and Pris to be alone."

At Stoney Ridge, Two Mom looked around the house that had a strange lonesomeness, but she knew someone who must also be lonesome. Two Mom turned to her daughter. "You ready, Pris?"

"Mom, do I have to go?"

"We should do this together, Dear."

"But what will I say to Alfred's parents? And his little brother?"

"I don't know yet, but they shouldn't be alone at a time like this, and neither should we." She picked up the car keys and her purse and headed for the door. Pris followed reluctantly.

* * * * *

Miles away, on Mad River, D.J. saw the lead raft pick up speed as it hit the first of the white-water rapids. The boat bucked like a wild horse, first riding high, then pitching straight down; twisting and turning as the power of the river gripped it. Icy spray doused everyone, sliding off the insulated wet suits.

But the rafters were enjoying it, D.J. knew, as their joyous cries echoed off the solid granite walls.

Connie called, "How's everybody doing?"

"Fine!" D.J. answered, hearing the same response repeated by the other three crewmen in the sweep boat.

"Then look sharp!" Connie said. "We're coming up on our first rapids!"

Tobin muttered behind D.J., "Those little things ahead? They're nothing!"

D.J. didn't agree. It hadn't looked so bad when he watched Brad's lead boat plunging through the white water, but as the second raft approached, D.J. was apprehensive.

He felt the increasing swiftness of the river. The peaceful blue-green water through which the second raft had been paddling changed into white water. Waves leaped up, slapped the bow of the blue raft and spilled inside. D.J. had been told that even though the boat wouldn't sink, sometimes it might be necessary to bail so it could be managed better.

The mighty power of the river increased dramatically. The raft was swept along faster and faster. Connie's commands kept the bow pointed downstream and off the boulders now sticking up in the water ahead. Through the spray, D.J. saw that the river was narrowing dramatically.

Connie shouted, "Swift water bend ahead!"

D.J. glanced ahead, and his heart seemed to stop dead still. The river made a right-hand turn. As the boat started around it, D.J. saw that the whole river seemed to be boiling with angry foam. Leaping waves hurled themselves against partly submerged boulders.

Connie's commands brought the raft in close to the right shore where the swift current marked a deeper channel. The tremendous power caught the craft and hurtled it downstream in a bouncing spray of white water that drenched D.J.

He glanced ahead through the water thrown up by the raft's bow as it hit still swifter water. The boy had brief glimpses of the obstacles he'd been warned were ahead. These included tricky currents, half-submerged rocks, brush, and other hazards.

D.J. mentally reviewed what he had learned about the makeup of the rapids and gripped his paddle tighter in anticipation of what was about to happen.

He felt the raft surge a little as it entered the deep, quiet water leading into a smooth V. This water was called a tongue. The rapids were immediately beyond, with all their treacherous possibilities. That could include a boulder just under the water with almost nothing on the surface to mark it.

"Whooeee!" Odell whooped as the raft began to go crazy in the current's powerful grip. "This is fun!"

"Great fun!" Renee cried.

"Fantastic!" Tobin yelled from behind D.J.

D.J. didn't say anything. He didn't think it was fun at all. He was feeling scared. Besides, the muscles in his arms, chest, and abdomen were beginning to ache from all the unaccustomed exercise.

"Reversal!" Connie called.

For a second, D.J. was confused, thinking this was an unfamiliar paddle command. Then he realized that Connie was calling out a danger in the water. A reversal or hole meant water suddenly turning back upstream in a wild, dangerous way.

Oh, boy! D.J. muttered to himself as his eyes sought out the hazard. He could see enough to guess that the upcoming reversal or hole was caused by a rock just under the surface.

The water flowed over the rock, but instead of going on downstream, the current plunged straight down. This created a whirling, churning area under the surface where a person could be trapped and drowned. D.J. saw a big log rolling and tumbling just under the surface as though it had been trapped there for days.

Wouldn't want to be overboard in there! D.J. thought, paddling mightily.

His darting, anxious eyes quickly picked out the other parts of the reversal. The current coming downstream was sweeping in from the right. The white water on top moved upstream to the left, forming a visible line where the two currents collided.

Easy! he told himself. *Don't be scared!*

Connie was wisely trying to avoid the reversal. During the instructions before shoving off, she had explained that a hole could flip a raft, stop it, or fill it with water.

Though he was watching the river and stroking hard in obedience to Connie's commands, out of the corner of his eye D.J. noticed the other paddlers. On his left, Odell was leaning forward, half-smiling, thoroughly enjoying the situation.

Behind Odell, D.J. glimpsed Renee. Her face was totally wet from spray that had leaped into the boat, but she also seemed to be enjoying the ride.

Tobin was stroking directly behind D.J., his eyes glued to the dangers ahead. Suddenly Tobin yelled, "Look out!"

D.J. automatically half-rose from his sitting position and swiveled his head to the left to see what had made Tobin yell. He glimpsed Odell and Renee also looking to their left. Nobody was looking D.J.'s way.

At that moment, D.J. felt a jarring blow to the back of his life jacket. The next second he was sailing through the air, still clutching his paddle. He automatically took a quick breath and hit the wildly churning water hard. Instantly, he was sucked under.

One thought rocketed through his head: *I was pushed!*

Chapter Seven

THOSE WHO WAIT

It was early afternoon at Grandpa Dillon's house. The old man sat alone on the high porch, gently rocking in his red cane-bottom chair. Hero was to the right, resting on his haunches, watching the eastern horizon. Stranger was asleep on the old man's left. Grandpa brushed a liver-spotted hand across his thin gray hair, staring with Hero toward the distant smoke.

Suddenly, Hero leaped up with a sharp, explosive bark. He plunged forward as though he were going to dive headfirst onto the ground below.

"Hero! No!" The sharp command stopped the dog short. He stood poised with his right foreleg up, frozen in action, whining anxiously.

Grandpa shoved himself to his feet with the aid of his Irish shillelagh. He was always a little stiff when he first got up. He used the cane to move as quickly as possible to stand over D.J.'s dog.

"What is it, Hero?" Grandpa asked, feeling the short

hairs on the back of his neck start to stand up again. It was a kind of fear he could not explain, but he sensed the dog knew something that he didn't.

The dog did not seem to hear the old man's questions. Hero slowly lowered his right foreleg to stand on all fours, but every inch of his body was tense, excited, ready to go.

For a moment, Grandpa wished he had not politely refused Brother Paul's invitation to come into town and stay with his family for a while. The big lay pastor and his daughter had reluctantly left, promising to bring any news of D.J. as soon as they had it. Grandpa had been left alone with the dogs and his thoughts.

Grandpa couldn't go to his daughter-in-law's home because she was allergic to the dogs. And the way D.J.'s mutt had been acting today, the old man didn't want to leave Hero alone. Besides, in a way he couldn't explain, Grandpa had a hunch he'd learn just as much from Hero as he would from any radio or television newscaster.

"What's the matter, Hero?" Grandpa asked, raising his eyes to follow Hero's gaze.

Hero still didn't seem to hear. Instead, he stood, every muscle alert, muzzle extended but not sniffing the air. He could have been a statue, standing so still. His ears, scarred from being ripped by bears and dogs in many a fight, were cocked as though he were listening to something no human ear could hear.

Grandpa glanced at his dog, Stranger, curled up beside the rocker. When the old man got up so fast, Stranger had opened one of his brown eyes. As Grandpa watched, Stranger slowly closed the eye and went back to sleep, his muzzle resting on extended forepaws.

Whatever was bothering D.J.'s dog certainly wasn't bothering Grandpa's. That made goosebumps form on the old man's shoulders and ripple down his arms.

The old man bent slowly over Hero and lightly touched him. "I wisht I could figure out what you're hearin' or seein' that I can't!"

The dog whined, but otherwise gave no indication of having heard the old man. Instead, Hero still stared toward the high country, tensed as though desperately wanting to rush there.

Grandpa turned and hobbled with the aid of his cane back to the rocker. He talked aloud to himself. "Whatever it is, I know it means D.J.'s got troubles! What could be happening to him right now?"

* * * * *

Plunging into the Mad River, D.J. felt the shock of the icy waters as he was sucked deep under the surface. Caught in the hole or reversal, he was tumbled wildly about like a rag doll in a washing machine.

For a second, he was confused. "Where am I? How'd I get here?" Then he remembered. "I'm overboard because somebody pushed me!"

D.J. had automatically taken a deep breath when he sailed out of the raft and over the water. That lungful of air wouldn't last long. He had to breathe, but which way was up?

He tried to see light, indicating the sky, but he only saw millions of white bubbles, surging past his open eyes. His ears were filled with a continuous sucking sound.

The churning caused by the violent mixing of the two

icy currents below the submerged rock kept D.J. suspended between the rocky bottom and the foaming surface. As he was whirled around and around, up, down, sideways, forward, and backward, D.J. could feel the cold seep through the insulation of his wet suit and into his body.

"I've got to get out of the water fast!"

He remembered Brad's instructions in a "man overboard" situation. "Take a mental grip of yourself! Tell yourself, 'I'm supposed to hold my breath, stay calm, and keep one hand on my paddle.' Thinking about the instructions keeps you from panic thoughts like, 'I'm going to drown. . . .'"

D.J. realized he was still clutching his paddle close against the chest of his life jacket. He forced himself to remember what else Brad had said.

"Maybe you'll be flushed out. That's always happened to me in all the years I've been rafting. But if that doesn't happen, take escape measures."

D.J. remembered them clearly and began to follow them. First, he tried swimming to one side. He hoped to feel the main current, which would draw him out of the hole. But he was thrown around so hard that he became confused again. He didn't know which way he was swimming.

"Try any direction!" D.J. told himself. He struck out his right hand in a swimming motion while keeping the paddle against the front of his life jacket with the left hand. He kicked hard.

That didn't work either. The recirculating wave, caused by the two currents meeting constantly, tossed him around and around.

"Kick really hard and swim downstream!" That was

another way to escape a reversal. But which way was downstream? All the water pressure seemed equal. "Or swim to one side," Brad had instructed. "Maybe the river will surge and flush you out, even if you're held a while."

Something gave him a glancing blow on the back of his crash helmet. D.J. remembered a tree trunk rolling heavily in the reversal seconds before he went overboard.

"The log! It'll crush me if I don't get out of here!"

He tried to force himself away from the danger, but there was tremendous pressure in all directions from the surging, blasting water. The boy had absolutely no control. He was tumbled wildly about in the enormous power of water and roaring bubbles.

Only twenty or thirty seconds had passed, yet D.J. began to feel light-headed. He realized his oxygen was being used up. From lots of summer swimming, he knew he could only hold his breath about forty seconds. Just a few more seconds and he'd *have* to have air!

Desperately, he kicked again and thrust his free hand out in underwater strokes. He felt the log brush against his right foot. D.J. automatically jerked his feet back toward his body, then placed the bottom of his tennis shoes against the invisible log. He bent his knees and shoved hard to push himself away from the log.

Suddenly, he was free of the hole! His life jacket made him pop to the surface.

Frantically, he exhaled and sucked in a great breath of air. A quick glance showed he was being rushed downstream. He remembered to bring his feet up so he was almost in a sitting position. He saw the smoky skies above the canyon wall and the end of the rapids. The river curved around a bend.

Where're the rafts? he wondered.

D.J. had a momentary sense of panic, then realized the rafts couldn't have stopped in the rapids. They would have been carried around the bend.

D.J. heaved a huge sigh of relief as the main current swept him around the curve, and he saw the rafts. They had eased into the quiet water of an eddy* to wait for him. He saw them breaking out lines for a rescue effort.

Connie's sweep boat was closest. The boy realized, *I've got to try reaching it! If I miss, I've still got a chance at the lead boat!"*

D.J. twisted his body as if he were riding a bicycle, aiming at the nearest raft. That didn't work, so he changed his sitting position into a full swimming one. He used his free hand to paddle toward the raft.

He swam awkwardly, still holding onto the paddle. He saw all the people in both rafts, their mouths moving. They were shouting encouragement to him, D.J. realized, but he couldn't hear anything above the river's noise.

Alfred's glasses were streaked with spray. He pointed and his mouth moved, but D.J. couldn't hear him either.

Connie threw a rope with a slightly weighted end, so light it floated. D.J. grabbed the rope and was pulled to the raft. Several hands grabbed his life jacket.

"Gotcha!" Odell cried.

D.J. was dragged across the buoyancy tube and into the raft, scared but alive.

Anxious eyes peered down at him. Voices asked, "What happened?"

D.J. glanced quickly from Connie to Renee to Odell and finally to Tobin. The look on Tobin's face made D.J.

decide not to say he was pushed.

"It happened so suddenly," he said, trying to sit up.

Connie said, "We can talk later. Brad's signaling for us to put in for lunch."

When the two rafts were beached at a nearby cove, everyone crowded around D.J. He insisted, "I'm fine!"

Finally satisfied that the boy was all right, everyone moved on to help with lunch preparations, except Alfred.

"D.J., what happened back there?" his best friend asked anxiously.

D.J. looked around to make sure nobody could over-hear, especially Tobin.

D.J. whispered, "I was pushed!"

"What? Who did it?"

"It had to be Tobin!"

Even though he was too far away to have heard, Tobin turned around and looked at the boys.

D.J. remembered the fleabite and the urgent reason for getting downstream to a doctor. "I don't want to say anything that'll delay us! I'll tell you more later."

"But if he deliberately pushed you—"

D.J. interrupted, "He'll claim it was an accident!"

Alfred sighed. "Probably so! But watch yourself! Maybe Connie'll let you change places with somebody so Tobin's not behind you anymore."

"Good idea! If I can get her alone, I'll ask."

In spite of his problems, D.J. found he'd worked up a good appetite. He and Alfred headed for the meal which Brad and Connie had prepared.

Four lunch boards two feet by fourteen inches had been set up as banquet tables. They rested on eighteen-inch high bailing buckets which served as table legs.

"Looks good!" D.J. told Renee, who was just ahead of him in line. "Breads, turkey, ham, all kinds of cheeses."

She reached for lettuce and sliced tomatoes before selecting the turkey. "A regular deli* spread, all right! Cookies and fruit at the far end! You're going to need the energy for this afternoon's run."

Tobin Swazey walked by with his plate already loaded. He leaned over to whisper to D.J. "You need a girl to tell you everything?"

D.J. started to answer, but Brad spoke up first.

"We lost a little time back there in the river, folks, so let's cut this lunch short. We've still got a long way to go before nightfall."

When D.J. turned back to answer Tobin, he had moved away. D.J. decided it was just as well. He didn't want to antagonize the sixteen-year-old any more than he already had.

D.J. eased along the lunch boards behind Renee. Alfred was muttering under his breath about Tobin, so D.J. turned around and whispered, "Shh! Not now!"

"But he almost drowned you, and now he's making nasty cracks!" Alfred whispered back.

Renee, unaware of the conversation behind her, turned around and smiled at D.J. "Tell me more about being a writer."

He shrugged. "There's not much to tell. I'm working as a stringer for the *Timbergold Gazette* right now."

"What's a stringer?" Renee asked, biting into her cookie.

"That's a journalism term for a part-time newspaper reporter who covers his own local area for a paper published somewhere else." D.J. added, "Sometimes Alfred goes with me and takes pictures for the paper too."

Renee sat down in the shade of a small tree growing back in the cove. "I've got a little instant camera, but I take terrible pictures! Could you teach me to take good ones, Alfred?"

Alfred didn't hear her. He wasn't listening. He walked off by himself, with a faraway look in his eyes.

Renee asked, "What's the matter with him?"

D.J. shrugged. "Oh, he's probably thinking about his family."

* * * * *

At Stoney Ridge, Alfred's seven-year-old brother and their mother heard someone climbing the steep wooden stairs to their small rented house.

Tag jumped up from the pale green upholstered chair. "Maybe that's Alfred!" he cried, his tousled head of short dark curls bouncing with his movements.

His mother rose from a matching chair and headed for the door. "It's probably your father." She was a pleasant woman with sad brown eyes. She wore her mouse-colored hair parted in the middle and tied back in a bun. She looked prim and proper, like an old-fashioned schoolteacher. She wore thick glasses like her son.

Woman and boy fairly flew across the tiny living room where Tag jerked the door open.

He was disappointed. "It's only D.J.'s mother and sister."

"Ralph!" his mother said disapprovingly. "O Hannah! Pris! Thanks for coming! Any news about our boys?"

Two Mom slowly shook her head, but she couldn't trust herself to speak.

"Come in!" Mrs. Milford said, shoving the screen door open. She had a tendency to talk fast when she was excited. "I got Brother Paul's message a while ago, but I can't reach my husband! He's off cutting wood someplace; I don't know where! I've been desperate without a phone or a car!"

Two Mom wordlessly stepped through the door and opened her arms. The two women embraced, trying not to cry and not knowing what to say. But there was comfort in not being alone—in having somebody who cared to share the fear and the pain of that moment.

Pris looked down shyly at Tag. "Hi," she said.

"Hi," he answered, standing behind his mother's gray skirt and peering out shyly at the nine-year-old girl. "My brother's not coming home anymore!"

His mother broke her embrace and swooped down on the little boy. "O Ralph! That's not true! Alfred's going to come home! You'll see!"

She glanced up, her eyes pleading silently with Two Mom as if to say, "Isn't he?"

Two Mom's eyes began to mist with tears. She swallowed hard and said with a conviction she did not feel, "Of course, he is! Alfred's with D.J., and they've had lots of adventures, but they always came home safely! They'll do it this time too!"

"Promise?" Tag asked, sniffing and rubbing a tear with the back of his hand.

The two mothers glanced at each other, anguish and pain making tears jump to their eyes. Silently, they gathered the two children together and clutched them tightly. Four sets of arms encircled each other.

Outside, a sudden gust of wind hit the tips of the dark-green yew tree and the sugar pine* that grew on either side of the steep wooden stairs. The trees first seemed to whisper, echoing the pain of the four people standing just inside the door. The wind increased, and the trees moaned.

Chapter Eight

TROUBLE RIDES THE RAFTS

The frantic mothers had no way of knowing that their sons were floating on a quiet stretch of water in one of Mad River's granite-walled canyons. The boys weren't exactly safe, but they were alive. D.J.'s overboard experience was fresh in his memory. He was nervous because Tobin still paddled behind him.

At lunch, D.J. had not asked Connie if he could switch places with someone. D.J. wasn't sure how he could justify his request without saying, "Tobin pushed me overboard and almost got me drowned."

What if Connie would not believe him? Certainly Tobin would deny the charge or at least claim it was an accident.

D.J. thought about that as he paddled automatically, vaguely aware that his muscles were a little sore. His mind wandered. *I wish I could figure out who Tobin's got me mixed up with.*

The sun had already passed over the western canyon

walls. Deep shadows were beginning to fill the river gorge when the two rafts came to their camp at a pretty little cove. A small valley extended inland through a break in the canyon walls. D.J. stepped ashore, sore from paddling, but considerably relieved that nothing had happened to him since his unexpected dunking earlier in the day. He walked over to Alfred who was standing near where the first raft was drawn up on the shore.

Alfred asked anxiously, "You OK?"

"Fine! Not a thing happened this afternoon."

Alfred worked his shoulders slowly, making a face. "I never did have any extra weight on me, but this hard work is going to wear me down to a wet suit full of bones."

"My muscles are sore," D.J. replied, gingerly flexing his biceps, "but I'll take that to the fires and being in that icy water."

"How about the fleabite?"

D.J. considered that a moment, then shrugged. "I feel fine, but I guess no symptoms would show up for several days anyway."

"By then, we'll be at Summit City," Alfred said. "You get your shots while I call your parents."

"Good idea! Dad or Two Mom will let your folks know we're OK! Boy! I'll feel better when that's done! Well, let's help around camp and then see where we're going to sleep."

"How about right by the river?"

D.J. shook his head. "Too noisy! I'd rather sleep back inland so we can hear if—if anybody comes prowling around. Besides, my dad always taught me to camp away from the river in case it rises unexpectedly while we're asleep."

The boy paused, thinking about his father.

*   *   *   *   *

At that moment, Sam Dillon stopped his car beside the country road near where D.J.'s grandfather lived. Dad Dillon balanced himself carefully as he walked across a narrow plank that had been laid across the creek, which murmured pleasantly, sliding over stones.

D.J.'s father passed the cottonwood trees now fluttering in a light breeze. He climbed the rutted hill toward the small frame house that was almost hidden in the trees. He wondered if D.J. would ever again take this walk himself.

The thought was so awful that the lumberman shook his head, forcing the idea away. Instead, he tried to imagine what his father would say.

I sure hope he doesn't give me any trouble, Sam Dillon thought. *He can be so downright unreasonable sometimes! Whoops! That's Hero's bark! He's heard me! And Stranger!*

The powerful logger called above the dogs' loud barking, "It's me!"

Grandpa yelled back, "You got good news?"

It took Dad Dillon a moment to answer, "No." That sounded so terrible that he added immediately, "Not yet."

Minutes later, Grandpa rocked in his squeaking old cane-bottom chair while his son sat sadly on the top step. Dusk settled slowly and peacefully over them and the two dogs, but Grandpa's hard rocking showed he was not peaceful within.

"By thunder!" he roared, driving the rubber tip of his

cane down so hard against the splintery porch that both dogs jumped. "I'm not a'gonna jist sit here like a bump on a frog and do nothing!"

His son sighed. "Now just what in the world do you think you're going to do?"

Grandpa rocked faster, his squeaking chair almost seeming to be in pain. "I'm a'gonna put on my boots, git me a hard hat, and go up there a lookin' for my grandson! *That's* what I'm a'gonna do!"

"You can't do that!"

Grandpa let out a bellow. "Why in tarnation *can't* I?" He rocked harder and faster. He only did that when he was upset.

His son started to warn, "Careful! You'll rock so hard that you'll—"

His warning came too late. The old, red, cane-bottom chair tipped so far backward that it fell with a crash.

Grandpa was thrown against the wall, his legs sticking up in the air. His overall pants legs slid up, showing he still had on long underwear even though it was June.

"You hurt?" Dad Dillon asked, leaping up from the top step.

" 'Course I ain't hurt!" the old man roared, rolling over on his side and trying to get his wire-framed glasses back on. "This here o'nry chair done throwed me, is all!"

He pulled his knees under himself, grabbed his Irish shillelagh, and began whanging it on the overturned rocker. "Dagnabit! What's the world a'coming to when a man's own chair treats him like a wild bronc does a cowboy?"

Dad Dillon tried to suppress a smile. "You sure you're all right?"

"Didn't I tell you I was?" Grandpa bellowed, stopping his blows on the chair. "I'm well enough to go help my grandson, that's what!" He shoved himself to his feet with the aid of the cane. "Now," he cried as he started toward the screen door, "you give me one good reason why I can't go a'lookin' for—"

His question was suddenly broken as the arthritic hip betrayed him. It buckled and Grandpa fell heavily, both dogs leaping out of the way.

Dad Dillon gently helped his father up. "That's why you can't go," he said softly.

The old man's blue eyes glistened with frustrated and unshed tears. He said fiercely through clenched teeth, "It's no good to get old! A man can't even trust his own body!"

Impulsively, Dad Dillon reached out powerful arms and engulfed his father within their mighty shelter. Neither man spoke, but their bodies quivered slightly with the sobs they refused to let come out in sound.

*   *   *   *   *

Far up on Mad River, darkness had settled. The rafters had changed from wet suits to casual clothes. After the evening meal, the rafters gathered around the campfire. D.J. sensed a strong bond of friendship growing among them all, except for Tobin. He still gave D.J. hard, cold looks across the campfire.

D.J.'s thoughts jumped to the germs that might be getting ready to strike within his body. He brushed that idea away.

Renee's cheerful voice interrupted D.J.'s melancholy musings. "Hey, everybody! Let's sing!"

"Great idea!" Alfred replied, firelight reflecting off his glasses. "Around a campfire's the only time anybody'll let me sing!"

The general good humor of the group was strengthened by the resulting laughter.

At first, D.J. was surprised at his best friend's words and actions. Then D.J. told himself, *He's probably just as worried as I am, but he's trying to keep his mind focused on something else. Wish I could.*

Connie produced a small waterproof guitar from a special case. The sad-faced Ray brought out a harmonica. Maybe the scar-faced man only looked mean; maybe he had a sadness inside, a pain that he couldn't share. Like D.J.

The people started singing. Everyone participated except D.J.

He didn't feel like it. His mind jumped about. He thought about the frightening moments when he was overboard. He thought about the fleabite and possible bubonic plague. But that didn't seem so bad now. There was still time to get to a doctor. D.J.'s mind leaped to Stoney Ridge, and then back to Tobin.

D.J. thought, *He threatened me, and I'm sure he meant it! But why? I know he pushed me overboard today! What if he does something tonight when I'm asleep?*

D.J. realized his family and Alfred's family would be praying for the boys' safety. A verse came to the boy's mind that Brother Paul had preached on recently. *What was it? Something about,* "When you pass through the waters, I will be with you; and through the rivers, they will not overflow you" (Isaiah 43:2).

There was another promise too. Something about,

"God is with you when you are with Him" (2 Chronicles 15:2).

D.J. told himself, *I'm doing my best to be with Him!*

That was comforting because it seemed only trouble rode the rafts, and most of it was heaped on D.J. He felt it was going to get worse. He couldn't explain that feeling, but D.J. was terribly uneasy. He had been in too many dangerous places not to recognize the signs.

In an hour or so, the singing ended, and people told stories. There was lots of laughter. Even the scar-faced Ray joined in. But not D.J. He had too much to think about.

A pale moon had risen above the canyon wall by the time storytelling ended. Conversation lagged. People stared silently into the dying flames of the campfire, lost in their own private worlds of thought.

Finally, Brad said good-night and went to his sleeping bag. That seemed to be the signal for all the rafters to produce small, lightweight waterproof flashlights. They followed the individual pinpoints of light away from the fire to where, in the daylight, they had pitched one or two-man tents, or unrolled sleeping bags provided by the rafting company.

In a few minutes, only D.J., Alfred, and Connie remained at the campfire. She rose and doused the fire, but didn't soak it so it would be easy to start in the morning.

" 'Night, boys," she said, and followed her flashlight into the darkness.

D.J. and Alfred didn't have lights, but that didn't bother them. They found their way to where they'd placed their sleeping bags. Like both guides, the boys preferred to sleep under the stars, without a tent.

D.J. didn't really expect any trouble from Tobin, but just in case, the boys had spread their sleeping bags about ten feet above Brad's head. The Swazey brothers had a two-man tent to Brad's right; Ray Hazelbury had his one-man tent to the chief guide's left.

Both boys removed their tennis shoes, shirts, and pants in the darkness. They slid into their bags.

Alfred promptly fell asleep, but D.J. stared up at the sky. There was some sign of smoke from the fires, but the stars were still visible through the haze. D.J.'s mind filled with many thoughts. Those included his father.

They boy asked himself, *Why doesn't Dad ever tell me that he loves me? Maybe because he really doesn't. If he did, why wouldn't he say the words?*

D.J.'s thoughts continued until the moon disappeared beyond the western canyon wall. It was very dark in the camp. Coyotes howled in the distance. An owl hooted close-by. Finally, D.J.'s racing mind slowed. He said his prayers and drifted off to troubled rest.

Always a light sleeper, he was awakened sometime later by a slight sound. *What was that?* he wondered.

He raised his head, ears straining to hear whatever had aroused him. The camp was in total darkness. Alfred snored lightly in the sleeping bag beside D.J. From various points around the camp, D.J. could hear sounds of other sleeping people.

Somebody was awake; D.J. was sure of that. But who? Tobin? D.J.'s heartbeat increased at the thought: maybe Tobin was trying to sneak up on him.

The sound came again. It was very faint, yet it was obvious that someone without a light was slipping stealthily through the darkened camp on D.J.'s right.

He tensed, ready to roll out of his sleeping bag and

yell or do whatever was necessary. He listened intently for several minutes, but the sound did not come again. Slowly, D.J. relaxed and went back to sleep.

Sunday morning he and Alfred got up and went to wash at the river. All the other men were present except the Swazey brothers. D.J. mentioned that to Alfred, who shrugged and said they were probably off by themselves.

At breakfast, Tobin and Odell still had not been seen. D.J. heard Brad asking Connie if she'd seen the Swazey brothers. She shook her head.

At that moment, Tobin came striding out of the little cove near the line of trees snuggled up against the towering granite walls.

Tobin walked straight up to Brad and said, "My brother—Odell—has disappeared!"

Chapter Nine

A HIDDEN VALLEY

Brad asked, "What do you mean—your brother's disappeared?"

"Just that!" Tobin replied. "I can't find him anywhere!"

"He's probably just gone for a walk."

"No, he's gone, I tell you! He wasn't in his sleeping bag when I got up, so I figured he was just off getting cleaned up! But I've looked *everywhere* and he's not around!"

D.J. remembered the prowler he'd heard in the night. That probably had been Odell. But why would he disappear?

Brad tried to reassure Tobin that everything would be all right. The rafters volunteered to help look for the older brother. D.J. and Alfred joined the search, moving off to the far right of the others. D.J. told his best friend about the sound he'd heard in the night.

Alfred shrugged. "Why would Odell go prowling

around without a flashlight? Now if Tobin had done that, I wouldn't have been surprised."

"Me either," D.J. agreed. "Let's hope we find Odell fast. This is the second day after my fleabite, and I'd like to get moving closer to a doctor."

The moment D.J. said it, he felt ashamed of thinking about himself when one of the rafters was missing. *But, he told himself, it's not selfish to take care of your life. I just wish we'd find Odell so we can go on.*

Yesterday, D.J. had learned that the two guides were always up well before the rafters who normally slept until about seven o'clock. The guides usually served breakfast around eight. The typical camp pace was slow, with gear being loaded around ten o'clock, when the day's run was started.

But not this morning. Everything was suspended while the rafters looked for the missing Swazey brother. They spread out across the narrow cove, looking behind bushes, trees, boulders, logs, and anywhere else a man might be.

D.J. and Alfred walked off by themselves, heading toward the cliff about fifty feet high and a quarter mile from the river. Some distance away, they could hear Tobin repeating his story over and over to the other rafters.

"I woke up about dawn and saw he'd left our tent. At first, I wasn't concerned. But when he didn't return in a little while, I went looking.

"I checked along the riverbank and everywhere I could think of! But I couldn't find a sign of him! He's just disappeared!"

D.J. whispered, "Alfred, I wish I could believe him, but I can't."

"You think maybe Tobin knows more about his brother's disappearance than he's saying?"

"I don't want to sound suspicious, Alfred, but there's something about Tobin that I just don't trust, especially since he knocked me overboard yesterday."

"Well, Odell doesn't strike me as the most honest-looking person I've ever seen. But then, I suppose that's judging a person, and the Bible says we're not supposed to do that."

"Hey, look!" D.J. pointed. "Is that a shadow on the face of that cliff, or is it a crack about three feet wide?"

"Can't tell from here! Let's go find out!"

The two friends ran past some brush and boulders and up to the stone face of a mountain rising sharply upward.

"It's a shadow," Alfred decided as the boys came within thirty feet.

"No, I don't think so! See? There's light coming through it!"

Cautiously, the boys eased closer to the cliff, careful of rattlesnakes and loose rocks, the most common hazards in the mountains.

"It is an opening!" D.J. exclaimed. "Almost like a secret passage right into the heart of this cliff!"

The boys ran forward, pushed some brilliant-green buckeye* leaves aside, and touched the crack which might have been made by an ancient earthquake.

D.J. cautiously peered through the opening. It ran back into the mountain about twenty feet, then seemed to open up into a meadow.

"I'm going to check it out," D.J. announced. "You stay here and get help if I get stuck or don't come back in a few minutes."

Carefully, watching for danger in the narrow place, the boy squeezed through. It was dark between the solid rock faces, but it got brighter ahead. D.J. pushed forward and stopped in amazement.

"Hey, Alfred!" he called.

"What?"

"It opens into a valley! Go tell Brad! I'm going to explore it for signs to see if Odell came this way."

By the time Brad, Tobin, and Ray Hazelbury followed Alfred through the crack, D.J. had checked around and returned to the hidden entrance. He held up a sweat-stained, gray cowboy hat.

Tobin exclaimed, "That's Odell's!"

"I found it right over there by that buckeye bush!" D.J. pointed and led the way into a green meadow.

The five people searched in vain for another sign, knowing now that the older Swazey brother had been there.

Brad instructed everyone to spread out and walk to the far end of the valley, which seemed like a box canyon. The whole area didn't cover more than five acres, so everyone could stay in sight of each other as they searched.

The first sweep yielded nothing. The five searchers came to the end of the valley and turned around. Brad motioned for them to move closer toward each other and walk back through the center of the valley.

Tobin and Ray moved well off to Brad's far side, so D.J. motioned for Alfred to join him. They walked up to Brad. D.J. quickly told about hearing someone moving about in the night.

Brad listened politely until D.J. finished. "Thanks for telling me, but right now, I don't see how that ties in."

"Could someone have kidnapped Odell?" Alfred asked Brad.

"I don't think so. There'd be no reason, though sometimes people on the 'outs' with the law do hide out in these mountains."

D.J. asked, "What kind of people?"

"Mostly 'pot' growers; you know—those who grow marijuana illegally. A place like this would be ideal for hiding their crops from the authorities. Or you get a gold miner working the river who resents having anybody around, even passing rafters.

"Once in a great while, poachers give fish and game people trouble. But I've run these rivers for years without a single problem like this one."

D.J. stopped suddenly, turning toward the other three searchers. "Look," D.J. exclaimed, "they're shouting and motioning for us!"

Brad outran D.J. and Alfred to where Tobin and Ray were bending over a downed sugar pine log in the middle of the meadow. Tobin shouted, "He's unconscious!"

By the time the boys reached the log and peered over, Brad had examined the missing Swazey brother. "His left leg's broken—simple fracture that we can splint until we reach a doctor at Summit City."

Tobin asked, "Why's he unconscious then?"

"Probably from the pain. I don't see any sign of a head injury, no concussion or anything obvious."

The guide looked around and pointed. "Looks as if he was standing on that log and he slipped. Caught his foot in the branches of this downed tree and twisted it enough to snap it when he fell sideways.

"Boys, would you run back to camp and tell the others? Tell Connie we'll need the first aid kit."

As D.J. and Alfred obeyed, D.J. was aware that the sun was riding high in the sky. Smoke from the forest fires was less than yesterday. The boy wondered if that was because they were moving downstream, away from the worst blazes or because the fires were being brought under control.

*   *   *   *   *

At Stoney Ridge's only church, everybody in the small logging community had solemnly gathered in the little, white frame structure. They sat together under the corrugated sheet-iron roof and the open belfry, pocked with thousands of holes where woodpeckers had stored acorns. The opening hymn had been sung; a time of prayer was next.

Sam Dillon was aware that others were stealing glances at him. This caused him mixed emotions. He was glad they were there—glad they had come to pray for D.J. and his best friend. But Dad Dillon also knew that some of those sitting in the sanctuary were secretly grateful that it wasn't their children out there somewhere in the midst of the forest fires. He couldn't blame them, yet it bothered him.

He turned slightly so he could see Alfred's parents and little brother. They were sitting across the aisle and two rows forward. There was a slight slump to Mrs. Milford's shoulders, but she straightened suddenly and looked up at the big lay pastor as he stepped into the pulpit.

Sam Dillon wondered if Mrs. Milford had straightened her back in hope. Unconsciously, he did the same, sitting up straight beside his wife and stepdaughter.

From the pulpit, Brother Paul Stagg's voice rumbled up from his massive chest. The building seemed to tremble with the power generated by the big man.

"As you all know," he began quietly, looking over the packed church, "not all of our children returned safely from youth camp yesterday. D.J. Dillon and Alfred Milford are missing."

Dad Dillon was aware that eyes again darted toward him, Two Mom, and Pris, on to the Milfords, then back to the pulpit.

The lay pastor continued quietly, "We're going to pray for D.J. and Alfred right now because we all love them, and they are part of this family of God."

Dad Dillon lowered his head, hearing the words echo in his mind, ". . . we all love them. . . ."

That reminded him of yesterday's short discussion with the lay preacher. "You've never told D.J. you love him, have you?" Brother Paul had questioned him.

Then, for no reason Sam Dillon could see, Brother Paul had asked, "Sam, did I ever tell you the story about my father's death?"

That still didn't make any sense to Sam Dillon. He'd have to ask Brother Paul when this was all over.

Sam Dillon glanced over at Kathy Stagg. She sat stiffly, red-gold hair cascading down both sides of her face. She turned her head slightly as a tear slid down her right cheek. Her mother reached her arm across the back of the pew and drew Kathy toward her. For the first time, Dad Dillon realized how much Kathy cared about D.J.

Brother Paul's prayers always began quietly, then rose in volume as his earnestness increased. "Lord," he said so softly that the word was almost lost, "we are gathered here in love to ask for the safe return of the two boys whose usual places are empty in this church today."

Dad Dillon didn't hear any more. His eyes began to feel hot and a mist formed over them. *I love D.J.*, he thought, *but I've never told him! I wonder if he knows how much I love him?*

* * * * *

D.J. did not know. He walked away from the river camp with Alfred, after Brad, Connie, and the others decided what to do with the injured Odell Swazey.

Alfred asked, "You worried because of what Brad just said about losing most of today while they get Odell ready to travel, or about going over Dead Man's Falls tomorrow?"

"A little of both, I guess. We should have reached Summit City and a doctor tomorrow. Now it'll be at least Tuesday."

"You'll be OK, D.J.!"

"Yeah, unless we lose another day or two in getting there. You heard Brad say that once his raft overturned in the whirlpool at the base of Dead Man's Falls, and they were trapped there nearly a whole day."

"Well, that won't happen to us, D.J.!"

"I hope not, but being short a paddler because of Odell's injuries, added to our inexperience—well, I just have a feeling we're heading for mighty big troubles!"

Chapter Ten

TRAPPED AT DEAD MAN'S FALLS

The next morning when the two rafts were loaded with all the gear securely stowed, Brad reassigned paddling positions. It was reasoned that Odell, with his broken leg, should be with Brad, Ray, Dr. Trotman, and Alfred. Brad didn't want to put the responsibility on Connie.

Toni replaced Odell on the left bow of the second boat, opposite D.J., while Tobin was placed behind her. D.J. remained at the right bow position with Renee behind him. Connie stayed in the stern.

D.J. was greatly relieved to have Tobin opposite him instead of behind him where he'd been when he knocked D.J. overboard in the reversal.

As they shoved off in quiet water, Connie said, "As most of you know, there are self-bailing boats, but ours isn't one of them. We're going to hit some rough water pretty soon. We'll have to bail to keep the boat under control as we approach Dead Man's Falls. I'll tell you when to bail."

D.J.'s mouth was soon dry with fear as the current quickly became swift. It was much rougher and more dangerous than anything they'd yet experienced. The boat bucked and plunged, sending the bow high, then deep into the cold river. Countless gallons of water spilled into the raft.

Connie called, "D.J., take a bucket and start bailing!"

D.J. carefully placed his paddle inboard and grabbed a white plastic bucket. He bailed rapidly, but more water sloshed in than he could bail out. In growing concern, he watched the raft fill. This caused the bottom to sink and the sides to come in, making the raft sluggish and hard to handle.

Connie yelled, "Tobin, help D.J.!"

Tobin reluctantly unclipped another bucket and joined D.J. He whispered, "You were lucky, being rescued when you fell overboard."

D.J. thought a moment about the wisdom of even replying. He said in a voice so low nobody but Tobin could hear, "You know I didn't fall! You pushed me! But why?"

"Just so you'd keep your mouth shut about what you saw back at the cabin—that's why!"

D.J. protested, "What cabin?"

"Don't play dumb with me! You could have another accident! This time, you might not be so lucky!"

D.J. started to protest again that he didn't know anything about a cabin or why he should keep his mouth shut, but Connie interrupted.

"Faster, boys! Faster!"

D.J. and Tobin obeyed, bailing in strained silence.

Gradually, they made progress. The raft slowly emptied and regained its shape. When D.J. figured they were about down to one more bucketful, he saw Tobin stiffen.

"Listen!" Tobin cried.

D.J. paused, resting the last pail of water on the now-normal bottom of the raft. "Sounds like thunder," he said uncertainly, glancing at the sky.

"Waterfall! Must be Dead Man's Falls coming up!" Tobin replied. He clipped the bucket securely into place and picked up his paddle. "This is going to be fun! Fourteen feet straight down!"

D.J. didn't think it was going to be fun at all, but he clipped his bucket so it wouldn't wash overboard. He seized his paddle and settled carefully into his regular position. With his knees securely under the rope thwarts as he had been taught, he started paddling hard. He saw that the river was moving very rapidly toward the thundering falls.

D.J.'s muscles ached from all the unaccustomed exercise, but he didn't care. The threat of going over a four-teen-foot waterfall was of much more concern to him. The river wound around a bend and into the fastest water D.J. had seen so far. He saw Brad's boat about a hundred yards ahead rushing along at tremendous speed. Then the sweep raft was also caught up in the powerful current and rushed headlong toward the lip of the falls. D.J. couldn't see anything beyond that; it was like coming up on the end of the earth.

He watched Brad's lead boat hit the top of the falls, then vanish.

"O Lord!" D.J. whispered as he wedged his knees more securely under the rope thwarts so there'd be less danger of being washed overboard.

D.J. tried to take his mind off the fearful sight rushing

upon him by remembering Connie's explanation that morning.

"Below a vertical waterfall, all the water's going straight down, below the surface. White, aerated, bubbly foam rises to the surface and floats back upstream. That can hold a boat because there's no surface water to blast it downstream. But Dead Man's Falls isn't likely to do that to us."

I hope she's right! D.J. told himself as the current swept the raft straight to the brink of the thundering falls.

The raft sailed out over the falls, seemed to hang for a moment in midair, then plummeted down.

D.J. felt his stomach lurch sickeningly. He had never fallen fourteen feet before. He sucked in his breath and held it as the raft plunged downward in a heart-stopping fall. He couldn't see through the water smacking him in the face. He couldn't hear anything except the deafening roar of the falls.

The raft hit the whirlpool at the base of the falls with a bone-snapping jar. D.J. felt a little giddy from being jostled about in a foaming whirlpool. He regained his balance and saw Brad's boat shooting downstream with everyone in it whooping joyfully.

D.J. was eager to follow the lead raft on downstream when the surface water blasted his raft free of the whirlpool's violent grip.

But D.J.'s boat did not shoot off down the river as the lead boat had done.

Instead, the second boat stuck hard against an invisible obstruction at the base of the falls. The raft bounced sideways and was caught by a monstrous white wave. The craft's bow shot into the air like a rearing horse. The boat flipped over so fast D.J. lost his paddle. Everyone was thrown out.

Oh, no! Not again! his mind screamed.

Then he was plunged into the foaming, frothy pool with the waterfall crashing down in an unceasing roar.

* * * * *

That afternoon after church at Stoney Ridge, Grandpa was sitting on the front porch, rocking gently and looking toward the east. The skies looked a little less smoky today. The fire fighters seemed to be gaining on the distant blazes.

Suddenly, Hero leaped up from his usual position of sitting on his haunches at the old man's side. "Bah-ooooo!"

The dog's mournful howl exploded so quickly that the old man nearly dropped his Irish shillelagh. Hero's muzzle quivered as the unearthly sound poured out in a long, wavering cry.

"Thunderation!" Grandpa cried, jumping up from his rocker. "Hero! Don't do that no more! You're spooking me out of a year's growth!"

"Bahooooo!" The dog's howl came again.

"Stop it, I said!" Grandpa yelled. "What's got into you, Hero?"

The dog didn't seem to hear. He took a fast breath and howled a third time.

Grandpa felt goosebumps running all over his neck, shoulders, and arms. He raised his watery blue eyes from the dog to look toward the distant mountains.

"O Lord!" Grandpa prayed, almost in a moan. "O

Lord! I know it's D.J., and I can't lift a finger to help him or Alfred, so You've got to! Please? Oh, please!"

*   *   *   *   *

In the wild whirlpool at the base of Dead Man's Falls, D.J.'s life preserver popped him to the surface like a cork in a bathtub. He came up alongside the upside-down raft. He reached out and grabbed the taut lifeline that entirely circled the boat just above the waterline.

He glanced around for the others. Connie was already climbing onto the boat from the other side. She still clutched her paddle, but the four crew members had lost theirs.

Tobin seemed to leap from the foam. He spat water and coughed, reaching for the lifeline. Toni and Renee bobbed up together.

They all scrambled onto the overturned raft as it bucked and bounced in an irregular circle. The force of the waterfall plunging down inches away forced the raft into a maddening spin in the center of the foaming pool.

Connie called above the noise, "Everybody OK?"

Her words were almost lost in the waterfall's thunder, but D.J. joined everyone in nodding.

Connie tried shouting again, but she couldn't be heard. She began using standard rafter's hand signals.

D.J. understood she wanted everyone to use hands to steer the overturned raft toward the four paddles floating in the whirlpool. The boy leaned over the flipped raft and began stroking toward the nearest paddle. It took some time to recover all the paddles. This delay concerned D.J.

Why couldn't our raft have stayed upright and gone

on downstream like Brad's? D.J. thought. It was already out of sight. *I can't afford to lose any more time! Oh, well, we'll be right behind them in a couple of minutes.*

He was glad when Connie motioned for everyone to stroke toward the main stream, shooting away from the falls. D.J. knew that first they had to get free of all this whirling water, then they would go downstream to a quiet pool and right the raft.

The first efforts to break free of the whirlpool at the base of the falls failed. The raft spun in a circle, bucking like a wild horse trying to unseat the five passengers.

The wall of water plunged over Dead Man's Falls in an unending cascade. The power of the water should have shot the raft right on downstream, but the swirling back current prevented that. Connie's sweep raft was trapped.

D.J. remembered what Brad had said earlier: "A raft that's upside down at the base of a waterfall can be held for anywhere from half an hour to a whole day!"

D.J. thought, *I can't afford to lose a whole day! I've got to get to a doctor! And Odell's got to have a doctor for his broken leg!*

Hour after hour, Connie tried every way to break the raft free of the whirlpool's grip. Nothing worked.

D.J.'s mind wandered. *Hope Alfred's OK. I'm glad his boat didn't get trapped here. He must be worried. Brad's probably having his boat wait downstream for us. Too bad they can't come back and help us. But we've got to solve our own problem.*

D.J. tried to take his mind off the frustrating situation. He thought about Kathy, Brother Paul's daughter. *Wonder where she is, and if she's thinking about us.*

*　*　*　*　*

At Stoney Ridge, D.J.'s stepsister and Kathy were sitting in the lay preacher's living room watching the news on television. Dad Dillon and Two Mom, Alfred's parents, and his little brother were in the kitchen with Brother Paul and his wife.

Kathy sat on the floor, leaning against a footstool in front of her father's big chair. "Nothing much on the news," she said with a sigh.

"Well, at least they're getting the fires under control," the nine-year-old visitor replied. "Pretty soon they'll be able to use the airplanes and helicopters to search for D.J. and Alfred."

Kathy's red-gold hair cascaded down both sides of her freckled face as she stood up to turn off the TV set. "My dad says maybe he and some of the men from the church will go searching for the boys when the fires are out."

Pris glanced up at Kathy when she turned around in front of the television set. Tears glistened in the older girl's eyes. Pris asked, "You like D.J. a lot, don't you?"

Kathy twisted her head away and looked out the living room window. "Sort of," she admitted.

"You used to say, 'He's cute.' I heard you say that, so one day I told D.J. and—"

Kathy spun around, her mouth flying open in surprise and embarrassment. "You told—? Oh!" She ran into the hallway toward her room.

As Pris heard Kathy's door slam, Pris asked aloud, "What got into her?"

*　*　*　*　*

At the churning base of Dead Man's Falls, another frustrating hour had passed with the flipped raft still unable to break free.

D.J. was concerned. *I've got to get to a doctor! Time's running out on me! I don't want to die of the plague!*

He tried to comfort himself by remembering the biblical promise he'd heard in Brother Paul's sermons. "God is with you when you're with Him" (2 Chron. 15:2). D.J. was beginning to doubt that.

D.J. raised his eyes. The skies were clear above the canyon's rims. He realized that the fires must be either far behind them or about under control. Then D.J. glanced down at the whirlpool that had held the raft prisoner almost a full day.

He looked down at the big, exploding, chaotic waves. *If we could just find where the current is that goes downstream, we could get out of this whirlpool.*

As he had for hours, D.J.'s eyes searched for the hidden jet stream. Facing south, he saw a small log that had been tumbling around with the raft over the hours. The log suddenly turned and shot downstream to the west.

D.J. spun around to face Connie. He pointed to the log. Instantly, she understood what the boy meant.

She gave the command, "Forward!" It was barely heard above the waterfall's roar, but five paddles dipped hard into the foam.

D.J. held his breath as the raft's bow touched the area in the water where the log had been seized by the jet stream. For a moment, the raft seemed about to be spun back into the pool again.

Suddenly, the boat shot forward so fast D.J. fell backward. He had to grab onto the lifeline around the buoyancy tube to keep from being washed overboard.

Someone whooped, "Whoooeeee! We're free!"

They were free of one danger but rushing headlong into a much worse one!

Chapter Eleven

THE DEVIL'S WASHING MACHINE

It was so late in the day after escaping from the whirlpool at Dead Man's Falls that both rafts put in at the
nearest campsite. The food and supplies in the overturned raft had been so secure in their watertight con-
tainers that most were safe.

After dinner, singing, and storytelling around the
campfire, Brad spoke up. "As you know, we've lost two
days from our planned schedule. I had expected to be at
Summit City by now. Our delays couldn't be helped. I
don't expect any more lost time, but you should know
the river downstream is worse than anything we've seen
so far."

Renee exclaimed, "We don't care! It's fun!"

Everyone agreed happily except D.J. and Alfred. They
just looked at each other in silence. The other rafters
were on the trip to enjoy themselves, but D.J. had a time
bomb ticking inside of him because of the fleabite and
danger of plague. To him and his best friend, escaping

down raging rapids wasn't their idea of fun, though it certainly was exciting and dangerous.

Brad's next words made D.J.'s heart leap with new concern.

"Tomorrow morning," Brad continued, "we run the Devil's Washing Machine. Its name is well-earned. Just beyond that, we'll reach Summit City where we'll get a doctor for Odell's broken leg and—"

D.J. sucked in his breath, afraid Brad was going to accidentally reveal D.J.'s health problem.

But the head guide concluded, "—so I suggest you all get a good night's rest."

Half an hour later, D.J. and Alfred lay in their sleeping bags in the darkened camp. There were millions of stars in a sky nearly free of any forest fire smoke. D.J. tried not to think about the germs that might be spreading through his body, but he couldn't help it.

"Alfred," he asked softly, "do you ever think about—dying?"

His friend's voice came quietly through the darkness. "No, not really."

There was silence between them, but it was the comfortable silence of good friends.

Alfred seemed to sense what was on D.J.'s mind. "You've still got time to get to a doctor."

"I know. But if we lose another day—"

"Don't think about it!" Alfred interrupted. "Brad said we'll be in Summit City tomorrow!"

D.J. sighed. "I hope so!"

There was another momentary silence before D.J. asked, "Does your father ever tell you he loves you?"

"Sometimes."

D.J. pushed himself up on his elbows to look toward

his friend in the darkness. "He *does?*"

"Sure! Doesn't yours?"

D.J. swallowed hard and slowly lay back flat, looking up at the stars. "No."

"Never?"

"Never!" It was such a sad, lonely word.

A coyote yipped in the distance before either boy spoke again. Finally D.J. whispered, "If I die on this trip—"

Alfred sat bolt upright in his sleeping bag and grabbed D.J.'s bag. "Don't talk like that!"

D.J. sighed. "Well, anyway, there's one thing I want more in the world than anything else."

"What's that?"

D.J. didn't answer for a moment. Finally, he said very softly, "I wish my father would hug me—he never does that—and I wish he'd tell me that he loves me. I mean, in words, so I can hear them and remember them forever."

Alfred didn't reply, so D.J. finished in a sad, lonely voice. "But—he never has, and I guess he never will."

* * * * *

At Stoney Ridge, D.J.'s father and Brother Paul were walking away from Grandpa Dillon's little house after making sure the old man was all right. The big lay pastor played a two-cell flashlight on the rutted way that led down to where Dad had parked his car.

Sam Dillon said, "He's taking it pretty well."

"Outwardly, maybe." Brother Paul's voice rumbled through the darkness. "Inside, I think he's sort of torn up. It's been days now without a word. Except he thinks

D.J.'s OK because of the way his dog's been acting. He's quit howling, just sits and looks toward the high country. I've heard tell of such things happening."

"It's strange, all right. But D.J. and that dog of his are close—closer'n I am to my own son, it seems."

Brother Paul didn't answer.

Sam Dillon went on. "It's also strange how something terrible like this brings people together." He glanced up at the moon riding high above the ponderosas. "Makes a person think a powerful lot."

"What about, Sam?"

"Oh, I was thinking that if I had it to do over again, I'd do some things different."

"You mean, in raising your son?"

"Something like that. It seems to me that fathers and sons often lock horns when they don't mean to. There's a tension between them that nobody wants. Like D.J. and me. But nobody does anything about it, and one day, it's—too late."

"Sam, the other day I said that someday I'd tell you about my father's death. Soon's we cross the creek and start driving into town, I'll tell you."

Dad Dillon had a vaguely uneasy feeling about what the big lay pastor was going to say. *But I want to know,* the powerful logger thought, *just like I want to know where my son is now.*

* * * * *

At the camp on Mad River, D.J. was listening to the low murmur of voices coming from the darkened Swazey brothers' campsite. D.J. couldn't understand the words though he wished he could.

Odell Swazey's broken leg was bothering him. It was splinted, but couldn't be set until they reached a doctor. Odell reached down to ease the leg into a more comfortable position on top of the sleeping bag.

His younger brother asked softly in the darkness, "You gonna make it?"

"I'll make it, but it hurts plenty."

"Maybe that'll teach you to go off prowling in the dark by yourself!"

The older brother ignored the sarcasm in Tobin's voice. Odell explained, "I saw that crack in the wall before dark. Nobody else did, so I had an idea."

"Yeah?"

"Yeah! I could see enough to know that there seemed to be a valley beyond the crack. So I got up early and slipped out of camp to explore by myself. I figured to be back shortly after daybreak, so nobody'd miss me."

"Including me!"

"I wasn't trying to keep it from you, Tobin! I just wanted to make sure what it was before I said anything. And I found exactly what I hoped for."

"You mean that little valley?"

"I mean a perfect place to grow our next crop of 'pot!' "

Tobin stirred in his sleeping bag. "Yeah! That'd be perfect! Nobody'd ever suspect it was there! But—how would you plant it, or get it out?"

"Helicopter!"

"Hey, that's neat!"

"But it's too late now. Everybody in the two rafts knows the valley's there."

'Maybe they wouldn't tell."

"They'd tell! It's too interesting a place not to mention

to somebody; maybe even the cops."

"Too bad!" Tobin stared up at the sky.

"Speaking of mentioning things: did you ever find out if that D.J. kid told about you setting the fire?"

"He claims he doesn't know what I'm talking about! But I think he's scared of what I'll do to him if he does talk."

"He doesn't strike me as the kind who scares real easy."

"Well, he'd better be scared!"

"You still thinking of him having an 'accident'?"

"Since he won't admit seeing us at the cabin, I've been thinking he needs another scare thrown into him."

"Like what?"

"Like maybe him having another 'accident,' maybe tomorrow when we hit the Devil's Washing Machine."

"Tobin, you scare me!"

"You don't have to be scared of me unless you cross me. But that D.J., well—he'd better be scared!"

Odell let the silence build up before he said quietly, "You know, Brad's right when he said earlier that rafting changes people."

"Yeah? How so?"

"Oh. . . ." Odell began, then stopped. "I've just been thinking that I'm not all that happy with my life."

"You're not?"

"Nope!"

"I can't believe that! And even if it's true, what're you going to do about it?"

"I don't know yet, Tobin."

* * * * *

Outside of Stoney Ridge, Dad Dillon's car pulled away from the creek near his father's house. As the car started down the paved road, D.J.'s father spoke. "Brother Paul, you were going to tell me about your father's death."

"So I was," the big man rumbled in the soft darkness of the car. "Well, there were thirteen of us kids. I'm number seven. My father was a hardworking farmer. Honest as the day is long.

"But like many men, he wasn't the kind to show his feelings. Never once did he tell any of us kids he loved us. Not when we were babies, not when we were growing up or getting married or anything. Not once did he say that to us, until. . . ."

Brother Paul's voice seemed to break.

Dad Dillon kept his eyes on the road, following the headlights as the car ground down the steep, curving mountain roads.

In a moment, the lay pastor continued. "My mother died right after the last baby was born. I was just about half growed then. The older sisters took care of us, and Pop never remarried. Well, like kids do sometimes, I thought my father was a hard, uncaring man. So we didn't get along well. I didn't much like him, yet there was one thing I wanted him to do. "Just one thing! If he'd once said to me, 'Paul, I love you,' I think maybe things might have been different between us.

"Well, one day we had another argument and I took off on my own. I was gone about three years. Never wrote home. Never called. Figured Pop didn't care. But I had one sister—the oldest—who knew where I was. So she called me when. . . ." His voice trailed off.

Dad Dillon waited awhile before prompting. "She called?"

"Long distance from Oklahoma to California." Brother Paul's voice was low and soft in the darkened car. "Sis said our father was dying, and he was asking for all the kids to come see him.

"I didn't have any money, so I hitchhiked across country in the dead of winter. Nearly froze. Nearly starved. Took me nine days to get home. When I got there. . . ." The big man's sentence was left unfinished.

Dad Dillon waited in silence, steering automatically, but his heart was speeding up as he anticipated the end of the story.

The deep, bass voice continued. "I was too late. The family waited as long as they could, but they didn't know where I was or when I'd be there. So they held the funeral. Afterward, when they were all sitting around, they told me what. . . ." Again, his sentence was left unfinished.

Dad Dillon didn't say anything. He waited, eyes on the mountain road, his mouth going dry.

The lay pastor said, "My brothers and sisters told me what happened in the last days of our father's life.

"One by one, Pop called them in—all twelve of them. He started with the oldest, and worked down, skipping me, of course, because I wasn't there. He told them all the same thing, and yet not one of them told any of the others until after the funeral.

"One by one, Pop held out his old arms and gave each kid a hug. Then he called each one by name, looked them right in the eye, and said, 'I love you.'

"Twelve times he said it. He'd never said it in his life, not one time, not to any of us thirteen kids. But on his deathbed, he said it to everyone—but me. I got there—too late."

Dad Dillon's eyes were starting to feel hot and moist, so he had to blink to see the road.

When Brother Paul spoke again, his voice was barely audible. "Sam, I never got my hug! And I never heard what I wanted most in all my life: 'Paul, I love. . . .'"

The big man's voice snapped off abruptly.

Sam Dillon took a long, shuddering breath. He let it out in a slow sigh but didn't say anything.

Brother Paul spoke again, but this time his voice was stronger—firmer. The rumbling power was back. "Sam, when you see that boy of yours again, I hope you'll remember what I just told you."

Sam Dillon didn't answer. He kept his eyes on the road; eyes now hot with tears that hadn't been there since his first wife died in an auto accident. He stared into the night, hearing the wind's lonely, sad sighing in the treetops under which the car was passing.

* * * * *

The next morning at Mad River, Alfred exchanged places with Renee so she could be in the same raft with her father. That put Alfred in the second raft with D.J.

He was glad his best friend was with him, though the rapids immediately became so turbulent the boys had no time to talk. In two hours, they were bouncing crazily in the middle of the wildest white water D.J. had ever seen.

He called to Alfred, "The Devil's Washing Machine is a good name for this place!"

Before Alfred could answer, Connie yelled, "Jump to!"

It was a command D.J. had heard often enough in the

last few days. It meant that the crew was to leap to the high side of the raft to keep it down so it wouldn't flip. Immediately, D.J. obeyed, but it was too late.

The raft smacked hard against a huge boulder. D.J. felt a severe shock wave pass through the boat as it rode up on the rock. D.J. was thrown forward, facedown. Out of the corner of his eye, he saw someone sail overboard.

D.J.'s legs, solidly wedged under the rope thwarts, kept him from going overboard. When D.J. raised his head, he saw a terrible sight!

A pair of tennis shoes attached to legs in a wet suit stuck straight up out of the water. That person was pinned head-down between the raft and the boulder!

But who was it?

Chapter Twelve

THE FINAL CHALLENGE

"Alfred!" D.J.'s anguished cry sounded even above the rapids' roar.

He tried to stand up to help, not understanding exactly how the accident had happened, but knowing the upside-down victim had to be freed immediately or drown.

It was almost impossible for D.J. to keep his balance in the raft. It rested at a forty-five degree angle, bow high against the boulder, the stern partly submerged. The craft was pinned there by tons of water pressing against it. The overboard person was crushed between the raft and the rock, facedown in the river.

D.J. reached out frantically and grabbed the upside-down tennis shoes. He pulled, but the legs were held fast by the raft. D.J. shifted his efforts to push the boat away from the pinned body, but it was useless.

Desperately, D.J. tried again, almost moaning in his anxiety. His mind tumbled. *How could he be upended and caught between the raft and the boulder?*

D.J. saw an orange life jacket bouncing downstream through the rapids. Instantly, the boy had the answer to his question.

The victim's life preserver had not been properly snapped. He was thrown overboard when the raft first collided with the boulder and bounced back slightly. The force of the turbulent water had stripped the vest away. Without the jacket's buoyancy to keep the victim's head up, the tumbling current had upended him. He was pinned facedown when the raft smashed into the boulder the second time.

"Help me!" D.J. cried, looking around for the first time to the others still in the raft.

Opposite D.J. in the left bow position, Toni was trying to stand up to obey. Out of the corner of his eye, D.J. could see Connie was shouting something from the nearly submerged stern. D.J. caught a movement behind him and swiveled his head in surprise.

"Alfred! I thought you . . . !"

D.J. turned to look again at the legs sticking up between raft and boulder. "Tobin!" D.J. breathed the name. "It's Tobin!"

Suddenly, the current shifted slightly and tore the raft loose. It slid off to the left of the boulder and bucked downstream through the foaming rapids. About a second later, D.J. saw Tobin's freed body slide off to the right.

The wild current caught Tobin and tumbled him mercilessly, end-over-end through the foaming white water. He was slightly to the right and behind the raft.

There was no time to think, only to react. D.J. leaned far out over the right buoyancy tube. He grabbed the first thing his fingers touched. Desperately, he pulled against Tobin's flopping left arm.

"Gotcha!" D.J. cried, leaning backward and bracing his knees under the thwarts.

He spoke too soon. The powerful water snatched Tobin away. Automatically, D.J. leaned out again, but couldn't quite reach Tobin. He was borne rapidly away into the whirling white water, his yellow helmet looking like a big cork in the rapids.

D.J. uncurled his legs from under the thwarts and dove overboard. In three swift strokes, he caught up with Tobin. D.J. grabbed for the shoulders but couldn't get a grip. Desperately, D.J. kicked closer and thrust his right arm around the unconscious boy's chest.

The leaping rapids made it difficult for D.J. to breathe. He couldn't see well either, for the waves sprang high into the air. But he caught a glimpse of the raft as it passed him.

"Wait!" D.J. yelled.

The boat, built with a flat bottom to skim the surface, was swept downstream faster than the boys. D.J. saw Connie's frantic arm signals to Toni and Alfred to slow the raft so D.J. and Tobin could catch up, but the current was too powerful.

"Wait!" D.J. sputtered again through water that leaped into his mouth and nose. But he knew it was useless. The raft vanished around a curve.

D.J. turned his attention to Tobin. The older boy was stirring, coming back to consciousness. D.J. realized if he let go, Tobin couldn't survive without his life vest. At the same instant, D.J. remembered the danger of foot entrapment.

He glanced fearfully downstream. The worst of the

Devil's Washing Machine was behind them. The water was becoming less thunderous—less violent and foaming. The river was also much shallower and, therefore, more likely to have hidden rocks on the bottom that could trap a foot and drown a person.

D.J. forced himself into a semi-sitting position, feet outstretched, toes barely breaking water. He saw another half-submerged boulder ahead and remembered to push off against it with his feet. He did fine, but the current caught Tobin and almost tore him free of D.J.'s grasp.

It's cold! D.J. thought as his teeth started to chatter. *We've got to get out of here before hypothermia gets us both!*

As Tobin's consciousness returned, he automatically began to struggle as any person would who thought he was drowning.

"Don't!" D.J. cried, getting another mouthful of water. "I can't hang on to you if you fight me!"

Without thinking, D.J. brought his feet down so he could concentrate on hanging on to the struggling Tobin. D.J. felt his feet touch the rocky bottom. *Good!* he thought. *I can stand up and get to shore with—*

The thought was jarred from his mind when something grabbed his left foot. Before he realized what was happening, the force of the rushing river spun him around. He felt a terrible pain in his left leg as it was held fast.

"Foot entrapment!" he cried aloud. From what the guides had said earlier, D.J. knew his foot was caught between two large stones on the bottom.

The next instant, the powerful downstream current knocked him off-balance. He fell backward, his free right leg breaking the surface; his trapped left one twisted so sharply D.J. yelped in pain.

The current forced him underwater. The life jacket popped his head up again. D.J. had a terrible choice.

If I let go of Tobin, I can probably reach down and free my foot! But without a life jacket, he might drown. . . .

His thought was snapped by Tobin yelling, "Let me go! Let me. . . ." He struck out wildly with flailing arms. He pulled free of D.J.'s grasp and floated downstream.

D.J. didn't see any more. The surging current again forced him backward and under the surface. This time, the life jacket did not pop him back up.

* * * * *

At Stoney Ridge, Grandpa Dillon had gone to the old shed with his son and Brother Paul to get an ax the lay preacher wanted to borrow. They'd left Pris and Kathy on the front porch with Stranger and Hero.

Grandpa was saying to the two men, "I never seen the likes of it! That there hair-puller has done sat like a stump ever since Sat'adee, staring into the high country. Ever' onct in a while he'll jump to let out a howl that'll curl your eyeteeth! But he's been quiet for . . . oops! There he goes again!"

On the front porch, Pris and Kathy were so startled at Hero's sudden jumping up and howling that they clutched each other in fright.

"Bahoooo!" The dog's powerful body quivered with the anguish of his mournful cry.

Pris exclaimed, "He's gone mad! He'll bite us!"

It took the older girl a moment to realize what was

happening. "No, Hero's howling just like Grandpa Dillon told my dad he's been doing for days! Grandpa says it means something bad's happening to D.J.! My father says he's heard of such things!"

Both girls watched in fascination as the scruffy mutt continued to howl, breaking off one mournful cry only to suck in a lungful of air and throw up his muzzle to bay at the sky again.

Pris whispered, "Something really bad must be happening to D.J.!"

* * * * *

At the shallow end of the Devil's Washing Machine, D.J. managed to get his head above water. He sucked in great gulps of air and shook his head to throw the water from his eyes. The yellow helmet made his head feel heavy.

The boy tried to calm his thumping heart. He glanced down. He was in chest-deep water so clear he could see his trapped foot. It was wedged between two large river stones. His foot was slightly twisted where the current had thrown him off-balance and pushed him a bit downstream.

His mind raced. *Big rocks, but maybe I can move them! If not, maybe I can get my shoe off and pull my foot free.* He glanced around, wondering what had happened to Tobin. He wasn't in sight.

Even in the insulated wet suit, the speed with which the icy water sapped D.J.'s strength surprised him. He felt himself weakening and his movements slowing. Whatever he did would have to be fast.

He plunged his face underwater. The shock of the

cold current made him want to gasp, but he held his breath. The life jacket's buoyancy made it hard for him to stay submerged. He bent forward, his head and shoulders just beyond his knees. He strained to push his hands against the rocks. He added his free foot, but that threw him off-balance.

Too heavy! The realization that he couldn't move the rocks was automatically followed by his second choice. *Maybe I can get the shoe off!* He stretched out his fingers. *Can't quite reach it! Couple inches too short!*

He jerked his head above water, gasping for breath and shaking from the terrible cold. The rushing, down-stream white water hit his life jacket and poured a steady stream into his face. He turned his head aside to breathe.

D.J. shook violently from the icy water. *Got to hurry! Got to get free before hypothermia makes me too weak! Got to find Tobin and help him too!*

D.J. took another deep breath and plunged his face under water again. He strained to reach the tennis shoe. His fingers just barely grazed the tip of a shoelace before the powerful current forced him over backward.

He came up more slowly this time. *I'm losing strength fast!* he thought. *I've got to reach it this time or....*

He submerged his face and grabbed his left leg with both hands, frantically trying to pull his foot from the trapped shoe. *Can't! Try pushing with the free foot against the boulder!* He strained hard, staying under until his lungs ached.

When he popped up for air again, gasping hungrily in great, ragged gulps, he had a frightening thought. *It doesn't matter about the fleabite! Unless I get free this next time, I'll die right here!*

He pulled himself forward against the powerful downstream current, thrust his face underwater, and again reached desperately for the trapped foot. It seemed he did everything in slow motion, and he knew this was the last time he'd have the strength to try.

Can't quite . . . reach it!

Underwater, he heard the gurgling sound of the rapids and saw the trapped foot—only six inches away! Five! Four! A little more. . . .

He stretched, pushing hard against the current, but it was no use. His oxygen-starved lungs made him surface, gasping for air. He looked wildly about at a world he might never see again.

His mind and body were numbed by the cold. *I'm going to die in a few feet of water!* he thought. *It doesn't matter if I've got bubonic plague or not!*

Out of the corner of his eye, he saw a movement. Almost powerless with hypothermia, not sure if he was seeing things or not, D.J. slowly turned his head.

Looks like . . . Tobin! Wading upstream toward me, but it can't be. I must be imagining things. Too tired . . . getting so weak. . . .

He closed his eyes, feeling the life jacket hold him up, feeling less pain in his trapped foot and leg. Then something grabbed him under the shoulders. D.J. opened his eyes.

"Tobin?" he asked weakly.

Tobin didn't answer. He plunged his face into the icy water.

D.J. felt hands on his trapped foot. He felt one rock move. His foot slid free. That's all D.J. remembered clearly.

Vaguely, as through a dense valley fog such as those that come to Sacramento each winter, D.J. seemed to see himself and Tobin floating downstream. Connie's raft was waiting. A lightweight heaving line sailed through the air and plopped beside the boys. D.J. heard Alfred yelling, "We've got them! Pull! Pull!"

Then, through the mists that shrouded his mind, D.J. felt himself yanked over a buoyancy tube with Tobin.

Some time later Alfred seemed to be peering anxiously down at him. Alfred looked strange because he'd taken off his glasses, heavily streaked with water.

Tobin looked up in surprise at Alfred, then cried, "Hey! Now I understand! It was you; not him! You're the one!"

Alfred asked, "I'm the one what?"

"You're the one who—I mean—you didn't have your glasses on when—" He stopped suddenly, having almost blurted out, "—when I burned the cabin!"

Alfred explained, "I can't even see ten feet without my glasses! In fact, right now you're just one big blur. Anyway, I don't have any idea what you're talking about! Let's get D.J. covered and then we can try to straighten this out!"

"Never mind!" Tobin said swiftly. "Just forget the whole thing!"

D.J. looked up at the scene and wondered, *What's he talking about?*

Connie's voice was crisp through the fog which was slowly clearing from D.J.'s mind. "All right, everybody! Summit City's just around the next bend! Get your paddles in the water and let's get to a doctor!"

D.J. tried to smile from where he lay in the bottom of the raft. *Just in time too!* he thought.

* * * * *

Grandpa Dillon had been rocking in his old, red, cane-bottom chair, watching Hero. For the last few days, the dog had stared toward the high Sierras. Sometimes Hero had whined; a few times he'd howled so mournfully that the old man's skin crawled with a fear he couldn't understand.

Not once had the dog seemed to sleep. When Grandpa had gone to bed, Hero remained at his post. When the old man came out of the house in the morning, the dog seemed not to have moved. He hadn't eaten and only rarely drank from the yellow plastic bowl placed by the porch post.

Slowly, as Grandpa watched, Hero's body relaxed. He sniffed the air, his long, black nose twitching. For the first time in days, his stub tail wagged. Then, with a kind of concentrated sigh, he made a couple of half-circles and lay down. His eyes closed, and soon he was snoring like a human.

Grandpa lifted his Irish shillelagh skyward and shook it in silent joy. His pale blue eyes filled with tears. "Thank You," he whispered. "Thanks!"

* * * * *

Late that afternoon, at the little town of Summit City which straddled Mad River, two cars and a king-cab pickup topped the last ridge and zipped into town.

D.J. and Alfred, standing on a high corner before the town's only medical center, waved at the approaching vehicles. D.J. turned to face the rafters.

"That's my family in the first car! Alfred's parents are

in the pickup! Brother Paul's driving the last car!"

Alfred pushed his glasses high on his nose with an automatic thrust of his right thumb. "Looks like everybody's coming! I see my mother and father and little brother! There's D.J.'s father, Two Mom, Pris, and Grandpa Dillon! And Brother Paul with his wife and Kathy! Look, D.J.! Isn't that Hero in the backseat of Brother Paul's car?"

"Sure is!" D.J. knew that his pet couldn't ride with Two Mom because she was allergic to dogs. "Whoopee!" D.J. yelled. "Everybody's together again!"

The three vehicles pulled to the high curb, and all the family and friends rushed toward each other. There were glad cries and tears and explanations that came in bursts like machine guns firing.

D.J. assured everyone, "The doctor says I'm going to be just fine! Odell and Tobin too!"

Almost everyone hugged D.J., except his father and Kathy. She grinned shyly at him, and he grinned back. When Brother Paul engulfed the boy in his strong arms, D.J. whispered, "You were right when you said, 'God is with you when you are with Him' " (2 Chron. 15:2).

Hero had been left in the Staggs' car, but after Grandpa and D.J. hugged, the old man opened the car door. The mutt sailed out of the backseat and landed in D.J.'s arms. D.J. was almost knocked down in the dog's joyful whining and barking reunion.

Grandpa said, "D.J., wait'll I tell you about what that there dog of yours done these last few days! You plumb won't believe it!"

D.J. ruffled the scruffy dog's scarred ears and whispered lovingly, "I'd believe anything good about you, Hero! You're the world's smartest dog!"

Slowly, a silence settled over the group. D.J. placed Hero on the sidewalk by his left leg. It was sore from being twisted, but it'd soon be all right. The boy straightened and looked silently at his father.

Sam Dillon met the gaze momentarily, then turned to the people who'd been on the rafts. "When Alfred phoned me while D.J. was in the doctor's office, he told about how you all saved their lives. I'm obliged to you. I'd be right proud to shake the hand of each and every one of you."

D.J. introduced Brad, Connie, Renee, and her father. D.J. saved Ray and the Swazey brothers for last.

"This is Ray Hazelbury," D.J. said, presenting the sour-faced man with the scar. "While we were waiting for you, I found out his wife was killed in an auto accident. He took this raft trip to get hold of himself again."

Dad Dillon gripped Ray's hand hard. "I know how you feel!" he said. "It happened to me."

"And," D.J. said, laying a hand on Odell's arm where it rested on a crutch, "this is Odell Swazey. He found a hidden valley that'd be great to see again."

"Glad to know everybody," Odell said, shaking hands all around. "But I've been thinking I don't plan to ever go back there. This trip sort of made me do some deep thinking. Maybe I'll find a new kind of work."

"What'd you do, Mr. Swazey?" Two Mom asked.

"Well, Ma'am, I'm not right proud to tell you what I've been doing. Ask me again a year from now, and I'll be happy to answer you."

D.J. continued, "And this is Tobin. He saved my life, as Alfred told you on the phone."

Tobin shook hands slowly, thoughtfully. "He saved mine first, so I owed him. Owed him more'n he knows. I had him mixed up with somebody else, and almost did a terrible wrong thing. But—well, I guess I found out I was the one who was mixed up."

Renee stood with her father's arms around her. "You still mixed up, Tobin?"

He smiled. "No, I don't think so."

There was an awkward silence before Brad said, "Well, guess it's time to go."

As everyone turned and began to move apart, Renee slipped out of her father's arms and shyly approached Alfred. She lowered her voice and said, "Before we go, uh—Alfred, would you—uh—write to me?"

Alfred was so surprised and flustered he stammered before finally nodding. "I—I guess so."

D.J., standing close enough to overhear, smiled to himself. Brad had been right. Something special happens to people on rafts.

"Well," D.J. said, "Thanks again, everybody!"

His father held up his hands. "Just a minute, D.J.! There's one thing more that needs to be done right here and now!"

D.J. looked at his father in surprise.

Dad Dillon's voice came again, so low and husky that it was barely a whisper. He looked at D.J. with eyes that glistened with a suspicious brightness.

"D.J., before God and everybody here, I want to do— and say—something that's long overdue."

D.J. looked at his father without understanding as he moved forward, powerful arms outstretched.

"Son," he whispered, "I want to hug you!"

Before D.J. could answer, his father clutched him in a rib-popping bear hug.

"D.J., I—I—" Dad Dillon's voice cracked, and he had

to start a third time. "Son, I love you!"

D.J. thought his father's hug was the nicest experience ever, and the words were the best he had ever heard.

He would remember them the rest of his life.

LIFE IN STONEY RIDGE

BUCKEYE: The California buckeye is a small tree commonly found on dry slopes. In the early spring, the buckeye's brilliant green leaves grow rapidly. They turn brown early and drop off in late summer. The ends of branches have pear-shaped pods that are very noticeable after the leaves fall.

CB: Citizens Band Radio, authorized by the Federal Communication Commission for ordinary people to use.

CEDAR: Incense cedar, an evergreen, aromatic, beautiful tree growing up to 150 feet tall. It has a cinnamon-brown bark with a soft, light, durable wood used for shingles and other products.

CONIFERS: Another name for the many cone-bearing evergreen trees or shrubs. Spruce, fir, and pine trees are conifers.

CRICK: A common mispronunciation of creek.

DELI: A shortened form of delicatessen, a store selling foods needing little or no preparation to serve, such as, cheeses, cooked meats, etc. Deli has also become a term meaning the products as well as the store.

DRY STORM: An atmospheric disturbance, such as, clouds, wind, lightning, thunder, etc., but without the rain or snow usually associated with storms.

EDDY: a small whirlpool or area where flowing water starts going backward or upstream and into a circle, as in a sheltered area of a river.

EVERGREENS: Trees that stay green throughout the year. New foliage must be completely formed before the old leaves are shed. The term is also applicable to shrubs having the same characteristics.

HAIR-PULLING BEAR DOG: A small, quick dog of mixed breed. A hair-puller's natural tendency is to go for the heels or backside of any animal, including sheep, cows, or bears. How D.J. and Hero met is told in the first D.J. Dillon book, **The Hair-Pulling Bear Dog.**

INCUBATION PERIOD: In pathology, this means the time between infection and appearance of the disease symptoms.

IRISH SHILLELAGH: (pronounced "Shuh-**LAY**-lee"): A cudgel or short, thick stick often used for a walking cane. A shillelagh is usually made from blackthorn saplings or oak and is named after the Irish village of Shillelagh.

JEFFREY PINE: Closely resembling the ponderosa, a mature Jeffrey smells like vanilla or pineapple when warm. The ponderosa doesn't have such a fragrance. The Jeffrey's blue-green needles tend to be denser and heavier, and cones are not prickly like the ponderosa's. The Jeffrey is found in higher elevations while ponderosas grow down near the foothills.

JUVIE HALL: A slang expression for juvenile hall, a security institution where young offenders (usually under age 18) are held when considered too young to go to jail.

KOKO: The name of D.J.'s bear cub. This story is told in the second D.J. Dillon Adventure, **The City Bear's Adventures.**

MOUNTAIN MISERY: A low-growing, fernlike mountain plant that gives off a bad smell when it is touched or walked upon. The plant is full of resin which explodes in a fire. Because of this, forestry people usually burn it to keep it under control. Mountain misery, also called "bear clover," has a pretty white flower which looks like snow. *Kitkit dizze* is the Indian name for mountain misery.

POACHERS: Persons who illegally take fish or game, usually on someone else's property. In this story, the land belongs to the United States Department of Forestry.

PONDEROSAS: Large North American trees used for lumber. Ponderosa pines usually grow in the mountain regions of the West and can reach heights of 200 feet. The ponderosa pine is the state tree of Montana.

'POT': A slang expression for marijuana, an illegal plant frequently grown in California's mountainous areas.

SUGAR PINE: The largest of pine trees. A sugar pine can grow as tall as 240 feet. Its cones range from 10 to 26 inches long and are often used for decoration.

THWARTS: On a river raft, ropes used across the craft to hold equipment or people in place. In this story, equipment was secured behind the last paddlers on either side of the buoyancy tubes and in front of the guide's stern position.

WALKIE-TALKIE: A portable radio with both receiver and transmitter, which one person can carry and operate.

WET SUIT: An insulated, rubberized coverall type of garment that covers the whole body except for the face, hands, and feet. A wet suit keeps in a person's body heat and helps ward off the cold in chilly waters.

THE EXITORN ADVENTURES

Visit the make-believe kingdom of Exitorn where you'll meet 12-year-old Brill and his daredevil friend, Segra. Their fast-paced fantasy stories will keep you turning the pages to see what will happen next.

Brill and the Dragators

Brill longs for his humble home when he is brought to the palace as a companion to the crown prince. The emperor and his son live only for pleasure and Brill remembers how different they are from his grandfather who lives for God. Will Brill and Segra be able to help the former king escape from prison? (6-1344)

Segra and Stargull

Segra and Brill journey through Exitorn, across stormy seas, and into a neighboring country seeking Segra's parents. Their adventures call for courage and faith as time and again Segra risks her life and Brill's to help someone in need (6-1345).

Segra in Diamond Castle

Segra is kidnapped and held prisoner by Umber in Diamond Castle. When her escape attempts fail, she comes up with a plan to outsmart Umber and end his war with Exitorn (6-1449).

Brill and the Zinders

Brill and Segra travel to Magra to locate the Zinders. Only the tiny Zinders can brew the special medicine needed to cure the plague that's spreading through Exitorn. But Prince Jasper of Magra is also searching for the tiny dwarfs. Can Brill and Segra find the Zinders and protect them from the sneaky prince? (6-1450)

D.J. DILLON

· ADVENTURE SERIES ·

The Hair-Pulling Bear Dog
D.J.'s ugly mutt gets a chance to prove his courage.

The City Bear's Adventures
When his pet bear causes trouble in Stoney Ridge, D.J. realizes he can't keep the cub forever.

Dooger, The Grasshopper Hound
D.J. and his buddy Alfred rely on an untrained hound to save Alfred's little brother from a forest fire.

The Ghost Dog of Stoney Ridge
D.J. and Alfred find out what's polluting the mountain lakes—and end up solving the ghost dog mystery.

Mad Dog of Lobo Mountain
D.J. struggles to save his dog's life and learns a hard lesson about responsibility.

The Legend of the White Raccoon
Is the white raccoon real or only a phantom? As D.J. tries to find out, he stumbles upon a dangerous secret.

The Mystery of the Black Hole Mine
D.J. battles "gold" fever, and learns an eye-opening lesson about his own selfishness and greed.

Ghost of the Moaning Mansion
Will D.J. and Alfred get scared away from the moaning mansion before they find the "real" ghost?

The Hermit of Mad River
D.J.'s dog is an innocent victim—and so is the hermit of Mad River. Can D.J. prove the hermit's innocence before it's too late?

Escape Down the Raging Rapids
D.J.'s life depends on reaching a doctor soon, but forest fires and the dangerous raging rapids of Mad River stand in his way.